CONTENTS

CHERISHED MATE

CYBERMATES

CANDACE AYERS

LOVESTRUCK ROMANCE PUBLISHING, LLC

This series is dedicated to my children.

Casey, Haley, Sam, Tucker, Owen,
y'all are my reason...

for everything.

Laila Bissett promised her best friend that she'd track down Gray Lowe and get him to apply for Cybermates, the new shifter mate matching service. She has no idea the sexy wolf shifter, a.k.a. Sunkissed Key's most eligible bachelor, is about to trigger some painful repressed memories that send her into full blown crisis mode. There's no going back for Laila. Either she faces some horrifying truths, or they destroy her.

Gray is not signing up for any silly mate matching service. Not when his mate just walked though his front door. But how is it that her wolf is so damaged, so traumatized, she doesn't even recognize her own mate when she sees him? Something happened to bury Laila's wolf so deep inside her psyche that, until recently, she didn't even know her animal existed.

Even if she never accepts him as her mate, Gray intends to help Laila. But to do that, he must coax a terrified wolf, hidden away for years, to overcome her traumatic past.

LAILA

Mimi leaned over the bar, her coconut shell bra barely containing her massive hooters, and wagged her finger at Parker. "Don't you dare, Parker Pettit!"

Parker's face was pinched in a forced smile that did nothing to hide the pain practically screaming from her eyes. "I'm not!"

Mimi shook her head and tossed a bar towel over her shoulder. "You'd better not. I don't want to be in the paper again. I'm still trying to live down the Sunkissed Herald's writeup on the men's room incident when Micky Hamish caught the head of his pecker in his zipper and Heidi had to call EMS to perform a penis extraction for the poor man. I don't need any more publicity."

"I said I'm not...so..." Parker glanced over at me and licked her lips, her expression more strained by the second. "...I'm...not."

I held up my free hand in a show of support for my stubborn-as-a-mule, lying-as-a-rug BFF. "Hey, you know your body. If you say you're not in labor, you're not."

"What are you doing?"

Oopsie. Parker was staring daggers at my other hand, the one rapidly texting her mate, Maxim. I managed to smoothly fire off the text before dropping my phone in the tiny pocket purse I usually brought along for drinks. "Nothing. Nada. Nilch. Can't a girl play Candy Crush on her phone?"

"*Nilch* isn't a word, and you better not be texting Maxim."

I scoffed. "Maxim? Why on earth would I be texting Maxim?" Hey, two could play the totally-denyin'-and-flat-out-lyin' game. You say you're not, so I'll take your words at face value."

Mimi leaned over toward us again—those double D's precariously close to spilling out all over the stack of bar napkins. "Parker, did that guy behind you just slip? Is there a spill back there?"

I glanced back and saw the guy looking down at the puddle under Parker's stool. Feeling my eyebrows disappear into my hairline, I looked back at Mimi with wide eyes. "Her water broke!"

Parker sat frozen, the fear on her features clearly evident.

Mimi grabbed the bar phone. "Oh no. No, no, no. You are not having a baby in this bar. No way, no how. I'm calling an ambulance."

"I'm not having a baby. I'm not having a baby. I'm not having a baby." Parker was staring straight ahead softly saying the same thing over and over like a chant. "I'm not having a baby." My friend was losing it. Seriously.

I glanced down at my phone to make sure my last text to Maxim had gone through. "Don't worry about an ambulance. Maxim will be here way before them." That snapped Parker out of her trance.

"You did text him! You traitor!"

"Jesus, Parker. Not in front of the baby."

"She can't hear yet... Ouch! She can't be coming already... Oww! I'm not prepared—HOLY MOTHER OF GOD!" Evidently the labor pains were getting more intense. Parker sucked in a big breath and shook her head. "No. No, this isn't happening yet. It's just not."

I whistled out a disbelieving sound. "Parker, the contractions beg to differ."

Face red, eyes bulging as she glared at me, Parker looked more like a troll than a sweet little bunny rabbit shifter. Not that she'd ever been described as sweet. "Just...give me some water. I just need some water to sip. I'm fine."

The atmosphere in the bar was tense. The music playing was too upbeat in tempo—far too jarring for a woman going through labor. We needed to keep Parker as calm and relaxed as possible. Mimi signaled to Sarah, who pulled the plug on the juke box and killed the music. With the whole place suddenly quiet, Parker's face turned even redder.

"I'm not ready to be a mom yet. I need a couple more weeks. I'm just not ready!" she grunted through a contraction.

I grinned and chanced losing a hand by reaching over and rubbing her back. "Yeah, you are."

The sound of wood splintering echoed through the bar as pieces of the door exploded into the room. "Where is she?!"

"Aw, Jesus, he totaled my door!" Mimi rolled her eyes and scowled at Maxim, who took no notice of her whatsoever.

Parker glared at me. "I knew you were a lying traitor."

I laughed. "Yeah, yeah. You'll thank me later."

"No. No, I won't. I'm not ready to be a mom. I have so much to do, Laila. It's too soon. What if I screw it up?"

"Parker, honey, you don't have a choice in the matter. That little bambino is coming whether you're ready or not. Besides, you've been preparing for this for nine months. You're gonna be a great mom. A perfect mom. I promise."

"I haven't even finished the nursery!"

Mimi winced. "I don't think that little one cares."

"I'm not ready! See?! Oh, god." She swatted at Maxim when he tried to scoop her up. "No, no! I haven't finished the nursery. I haven't finished setting up Cybermates! I'm not prepared for her arrival."

To calm her down, and to avoid having to listen to any more of her protests, I threw myself on the blade. "I'll finish the nursery."

"Put me down, Max!" She hesitated. "Wait. You will?"

I nodded. "Uh-huh. I'll do it tomorrow. It'll be all ready for baby Stella when she comes home."

"What about Cybermates? You'll finish getting the site up and running, too?"

I wrinkled my nose. Mimi snorted. "Um, yeah, sure. Of course. Whatever. I'll do whatever needs doing."

"And you'll go by Gray Lowe's and make him finish his questionnaire?"

I sighed. "Gray... Yeah, yeah, whatever."

"And you'll meet with Dylan? He's the tech guy coming down from Miami to help with the website."

"Yes, Parker."

"And make sure Gray fills it out completely. I mean, don't leave until he does. He's been avoiding me."

"I will."

"Okay, great." She turned to Maxim. "I'm ready, babe."

Maxim scooped her up into his arms. His face was a sheet of pure panic, but he moved slowly and carefully, as though he was carrying the most precious thing in the world to him—because, well, he was. "Okay, to the hospital we go."

"Oh, wait!" She turned to me. "The appointment with Dylan is tomorrow at Latte Love. And I'm serious about Gray. You may have to lean on him a bit. I need a catch like him to draw in the ladies, even if he doesn't want a mate."

I just waved her off as Mimi slid me a shot of whiskey. "She just hoodwinked you."

I shook my head as I watched my best friend and her mate leave and head off to the hospital. "You didn't happen to write all that down, did you, Mimi?"

Mimi's snicker wasn't appreciated, but she refilled my glass as soon as I threw back the shot, so I forgave her. She even left the bottle between us. "I remember the part about you getting to lean on Gray. Which makes you one lucky lady. Every single woman on this island has been trying to lean on something of his—anything of his. That man is fine."

I leaned my elbow against the bar and rested my chin on my fist. "I also get finish a nursery, set up a mate matching website, and be Parker's junior assistant."

"What a con artist." Mimi motioned for the music to be turned back on as Sarah mopped up the "spill" under Parker's chair. In seconds, Mimi's Cabana was back to normal as though nothing had ever happened.

Only, I was suddenly shouldering a huge chore list. I took the liberty of pouring myself another shot before pulling money out of my pocket purse.

"Leaving already?"

"There's no way I'm missing that baby being born. I just let them leave first so I didn't have to hear Maxim and Parker bicker in the delivery room. He's convinced that even the doctor shouldn't be allowed to see Parker's vagina. I hope they have it all sorted out by the time I get there."

"Trust me, no one watching a baby coming out of a hoo-hah is finding anything sexy about it."

I shrugged. "I have no intention of being on that end. I'll be on the hand-holding end."

"Let me know what room they end up in. I want to send flowers."

"Will do."

I strolled out of the bar, feeling excited about the baby, but not so much about any of the other chores on Parker's to-do list. I'd never met Gray Lowe, but I'd heard plenty about Grace's somewhat mysterious, reportedly quite handsome, big brother. He was highly sought after by the single women of the island who considered him Sunkissed Key's most eligible bachelor.

He was also a wolf shifter—like me.

Well, not like me. I sighed. No one was like me.

GRAY

I drove to the south end of Main Street, all the way down to the southernmost tip of the island, and pulled my truck into the parking lot of the storefront space that contained the office formerly known as P.O.L.A.R. The Sunkissed Key branch of the shifter private ops organization was now defunct—disbanded in an act of retaliation when my brother-in-law had the audacity to choose my sister as his mate rather than go through with the marriage that had been prearranged for him at birth.

Since I was also out of a job after having been screwed by the government agency I had been working for, the ex-P.O.L.A.R. team and I were setting up a new business venture together. We were still deciding on a name, but seeing as how I was not a polar bear shifter, the acronym P.O.L.A.R. was a no-go.

"About fucking time." Serge was waiting for me out front holding two coffees from Latte Love, the island's best coffee shop. He handed me one.

"I'm on time, asshole." I glanced at my watch to be sure before taking the coffee. "Early, actually."

He turned and led the way into the office. "Do you know how much time I've been missing with my mate, dealing with all of this?"

"Hey, a startup is always a lot of work. It won't ease up until we get it off the ground and iron out any kinks either."

The "all of this" Serge was referring to was the work that had to go into removing P.O.L.A.R.'s presence from the building. The organization had long-reaching arms and anything put in by them needed to be torn back out. Maybe it was my years with the CIA, maybe it was my upbringing, probably it was a combination of both, but I didn't trust anyone or anything—especially not a government agency.

"I doled out thousands of dollars in tech fees and spent days in here going over every inch of this place, making sure there was nothing left behind. I don't know if I've ever been more bored in my life."

Grinning, I just shrugged. "You're talking to the man shot full of holes who stowed away on a Cuban fishing vessel for over a month to keep a low profile. The same man who's been forcibly put on medical leave by his sister. I can promise you that I've been more bored than you have."

"What a sob story. Boo-hoo." He gestured around the completely bare office. "It's empty."

"The wiring?"

"Redone."

"Walls?"

With a mighty sigh, he put his hands on his hips and turned to face me. "You think I'm an amateur? Redone. Everything's been redone."

Reaching into my pocket, I pulled out a small gadget I usually kept on me, unfolded it, extended the scanner, and started the tedious process of running it over the floor and walls, looking for any type of hidden cameras, listening devices, GPS trackers, and other "spy tools."

Serge raised a brow, crossed his arms over his chest, and watched me until I was finished. "Neurotic, much?"

"You do remember where I worked, right? Neurosis can save asses."

"I'll use that for my next tattoo."

"There's a reason I am the way I am. Nothing wrong with double-

7

checking things to ensure our plans don't crash and burn before we even get them off the ground."

"Are there still people from your past that we can expect to show up?"

"Honestly, I don't know." I folded the tool back up and put it away. "I don't think so. They burned me and left me to rot. They've washed their hands clean of me. I don't expect trouble, but there's a long line of shady characters that I've managed to piss off through the years."

"Another reason your name will be left off any and all paperwork. If we can avoid drawing unwanted attention, I'd like to do just that." Serge grunted. "So, what's the prognosis, doc? All clear to start bringing in our own equipment, now? We've got an entire office to put back together."

I nodded. "I'll write a check for my part of the costs."

"Damn straight, you will. We had a perfectly functioning office before you came in with all your talk about espionage."

"Dude, go home to your mate. You need to get laid, man. You're turning into a whiny bitch."

He growled. "Hannah hasn't left Parker's side since she went into labor. By the way, I've gotten a few texts from Hannah about how worried Grace is that I'm going to, ahem, *allow* you to be put in the path of danger."

Groaning, I shook my head and started toward the door. "My sister..."

"Yeah, she was pretty traumatized when she found out you'd been shot. She's pushing hard for you to get a nice desk job, like in a quiet museum somewhere."

"Ironically, a boring desk job would kill me faster and inflict far more pain than a bullet."

Serge took a gulp of coffee. "She's pretty protective."

"I'll have a talk with her. She's not the same after she came to Sunkissed Key to find me. She's so worried that I'm going to end up dead that she's practically killing me herself—by suffocation."

"There are dangers to what we do, sure." Serge shrugged. "We're not humans, though. Chances are slim that any of us are going to die from a little gunshot wound."

The ache in my chest could attest to that. Grace didn't know the full story—I'd been shot multiple times, bullets piercing vital organs, and barely came away with my life. "Our private security firm isn't going to be anywhere near as dangerous as what either of us used to do."

"That's the plan, anyway. I promised Hannah."

His mate would be safe, as far as I was concerned. Everyone would be. Nothing about our new business venture was anywhere near as risky as the work we'd done before. Our new company would provide private security—consulting, risk assessment, checking for potential vulnerabilities at businesses or residences, installing security systems, and one-on-one bodyguard services. Okay, there was still a minor risk when playing bodyguard to a VIP, but most of the time, just carrying an air of menace and a tough, no-nonsense demeanor was deterrent enough. Plus, for the first time, we had full veto power over cases—we chose which to accept and which to turn down.

"So, let's get this place set up." I slapped him on the back and we headed out the back door. "What the hell have you been waiting on, slacker?"

I heard the massive growl a half second before I felt his body slam into my back. I rolled and jabbed an elbow into the side of his rib cage just as he landed an uppercut to my chin.

"Fuck, I get why the guys used to beat the shit out of me when they were frustrated with their mates, now." Serge, grunting, tried to land another blow and, instead, got a fist in the gut.

I got out from under him, laughing but hurting. I was healed on the outside, but my body was still too tender on the inside for fighting. "I deserved that, I guess." As shifters, both with large, dominant animals inside, it was natural for us to have a go at one another once in a while. Brawling kept our animals steady and grounded.

Serge swiped some sand at me and growled. "If our mates abandon us every time one of them gets pregnant or goes into labor, we're going to fucking tear each other up."

9

"I don't have a dog in that fight, brother."

"Give it time."

I scoffed at the thought. I was in no shape for a mate. I didn't even date, despite the fact that the island seemed to be crawling with ready and willing women. I didn't need that complication. Not only was I not completely healed physically, there were still mental blocks I had to work through, as well.

"By the way, did Parker get to you before she went into labor?"

I brushed sand off of my clothes and shook my head. "No thank god, but it wasn't for lack of trying. That woman is like a bloodhound. Fortunately, I was able to dodge her. Hopefully she'll be too busy with the baby in the coming months to follow me around waving her little forms in my face."

He laughed and shoved off the ground. Standing tall, he held out his fist and I bumped mine against his. "No hard feelings?"

"Hey, no worries. You need my help setting anything up?"

He shook his head. "Nah. Alexei and Dmitry are taking charge of that. Actually, I think I'll stick around and help. I need something to do to distract me from the fact that I've been abandoned by my mate until Parker gives birth."

3

LAILA

*J*ammie's Salon was owned and run by Jammie herself. Seventy-something, wrinkle-free, and boasting a head full of hot pink hair, the woman was a force to be reckoned with. No one knew her real name, but the story was that she'd been nicknamed as a youngster by a babysitter for her love of strawberry jam. Even her salon reflected her bubbly, bright, and upbeat personality, a trait that ensured repeat clients and low staff turnover. I could personally vouch for the fact that Jammie was a great employer.

I'd worked as a stylist at Jammie's since I'd graduated from Sunshine School of Cosmetology at the age of twenty-two, so for almost eight years. Even though I was pushing thirty, I was one of the youngest here. Besides Jammie, there were a few other seventy-somethings, still kicking ass and learning new tricks daily. Margie, a senior citizen with a blue streak through her spiked snow-white locks, was the colorist. She was known for doing the best dye jobs on the island. Kitty, also a senior, had ebony skin and short copper curls. Kitty had magic fingers when it came to intricate styling like updos and braiding. Prom hair? Go to Kitty. New color? See Margie. And for a cut— whether you wanted a trendy, cutting edge 'do or a classic, timeless style—I was your girl.

October worked next to me—she was the baby. Fresh out of high school with poker straight black hair, she was still finding her groove and learning what she was best at. I'd seen a few styles that she'd done. They were amazing. The girl had true talent. Her black, stiletto nails, black lipstick, and dark eyeshadow were alarming to some clients who came in, like Mary Beth Jones, a local preacher's wife.

I kept having to remind Mary Beth, who was currently sitting in my chair, to keep her head straight. She couldn't stop glancing at October, whose name I wasn't sure was given at birth or at puberty. I was almost at my wit's end and ready to smack her upside the head with a round brush when she finally spoke up.

"I think I'd like my hair like hers."

October looked up from her client's head and raised her eyebrows. Okay, that took the room by surprise. Mary Beth had light-brown curls that were so tightly wound they resembled mattress springs.

"That color, you mean?" I prayed she meant the color, not the style. I'd be happy to see her go jet black. She'd look a little edgier than was her norm, but the contrast would be striking.

"I don't mean the color. Not the color. I want it straight like that. And shiny. It's so shiny." *Oh, kill me now!* Then she threw sod on my coffin. "With bangs. You can give me bangs, right?"

Mary Beth was in for her routine monthly trim. It was a thirty-minute ordeal from start to finish, including a shampoo and a blowout. She always wanted the same thing. A trim. Always a trim. She'd never even gone for the layers I'd tried for years to give her. Suddenly, she decided to go straight and have bangs cut in? I wanted to cry. It would take hours to transform Shirley Temple circa 1936 to Cher circa 1976.

To be fair, my mood wasn't only in response to Mary Beth. I hated leaving Parker. Her new baby, Stella, was a beautiful little baby girl, my goddaughter, and basically my niece—not by blood, but by heart. My heart was with the two of them right now. I wanted my body to be there, too, but I had a laundry list of things to do. Unfortunately, one of them was showing up for work and setting a good example of adulting for my new goddaughter.

"Well, Laila? Can you do it?"

It was at that moment I noticed the entire salon had gone silent. Completely. You could hear a pin drop. Jammie had even stopped working on Carolina Montgomery's perm. Eyes went from Mary Beth's corkscrew curls to me and back again. I took a deep breath and was just about to tick off all the reasons on my fingers and toes that it was a bad idea when October spoke.

"It's a wig. No one's hair is this straight."

"Oh." Mary Beth deflated and her shoulders slumped in the chair. "I was just hoping for something...*different*. To spice things up in the... well, you know where." She winked at me. Jesus, Mary, and Joseph, she couldn't even say the word bedroom.

Margie's snort from across the salon echoed through the room. "You want to spice things up? C'mon over here, sweetheart, and I'll make you a redhead, the undercarriage, too. Pastor Steve won't know what hit him."

Cheeks aflame, Mary Beth stuck her nose back in her *Women's Week* magazine and acted like the whole thing had never happened. Feeling guilty, I completed her trim and blowout, and when I was done, I leaned down and took her hand. "I'll tell you what, Mary Beth. Go home and think this over. If you decide you truly want to make a drastic change, give me a call and I'll carve out a block of time and straighten your hair with a flat iron. That way, you can test it out first and see how you like it. No charge."

October shook her head at me when the preacher's wife left the salon. "The look on your face for a second... I thought you were going to go all Sweeny Todd on sweet Mary Beth."

I let my head fall back as I sank into my empty chair. "It wasn't her. Although, I was terrified for a second that I was going to have to try to straighten her ringlets, one by one, in the fifteen minutes we had left."

Jammie, having set Carolina Montgomery under the dryer, shuffled over. "What's wrong, honey? You don't seem yourself today."

"Parker had her baby last night—Stella. I hate that I can't be with her twenty-four hours a day. I have to go straight over to her house after work to finish her nursery, too." I forced myself to stop pouting and shook out my hands. "I'm just in a funk."

"You know what I do when I'm in a funk?" Kitty piped up. "I like to have a big bottle of wine and remember what a goddamn good time I am."

Margie nodded. "She's not lying. It's one of those Costco-sized bottles."

I laughed. "Maybe I'll try that. After I finish the nursery and meet with the computer guy. And stop by Gray Lowe's house to get him to fill out some questionnaire for Parker's new dating service."

October fanned herself. "Gray Lowe? Holy hotness. And you're complaining? The teachers at my high school used to go on and on about him. I thought it was all old-lady hormones until I saw him with my own eyes. It was at the beach one day last summer. Oh my god, Adonis in the flesh!"

I scrunched my face up. "He's old enough to be your...I don't know...older uncle?"

Jammie just giggled. "Old-lady hormones. I've got those in spades, and I can tell you, it's not just hormones with Gray Lowe. He's a hot fudge sundae with whipped cream and a cherry on top—and extra HOT fudge, if you know what I mean." She winked. "That man can take my cherry any time he wants."

"Your cherry's been gone for half a century." Frannie stuck her head out of her room in the back. "Who the hell you tryin' to kid?" Even though she and Jammie had been friends since grade school, Frannie had only just started working at Jammie's Salon. As our newest team member, she fit right in with the rest of us.

"Gray Lowe is the hottest prospect on this island. Every girl wants a piece of Sunkissed Key's most eligible bachelor. I heard he doesn't date, though. Although that doesn't stop women from trying." October patted her client on the shoulder and winked at her through her mirror. "Am I right, Lucille?"

Lucille, a ninety-something with a sparse, wispy white cloud of hair that slightly resembled a cotton ball, nodded emphatically. "Oh

14

yes. I know that young man. He's dreamy, alright. With a tight butt, too."

My next client shuffled in and I stood to greet him with a smile. "Mr. Mathews, how are you today?"

"I hope I'm not interrupting any juicy gossip, ladies." Grinning at each of us, the elderly man slowly made his way to my chair and sank into it. "Don't stop the tittle-tattle on my account."

Anyone who had lived on Sunkissed Key more than a month knew not to gossip about anything private in front of Mr. Mathews. Not unless you wanted it spread across the entire state of Florida. He was *the* mouth of the south.

"We were just talking desserts, Mr. Mathews. Got any secret family recipes you'd care to share?"

Clearly disappointed, he sank into his napping position and grunted. "Secrets aren't meant to be shared, honey."

Carolina Montgomery, who was still sore at him for flapping his gums about her and the high school gym teacher being seen leaving the Bogart & Bacall Inn on Toucan Boulevard only minutes apart even though neither of them had any discernible reason to be checking in or out of a hotel at midday on a Tuesday, nearly snapped the hood off the dryer trying to get out from under it fast enough to respond to the old man's comments. Jammie saw an argument coming and used herself as a physical barrier between the two clients.

"Now, now, Carolina, don't mess up your perm. Sit back and relax."

I slipped into the back room on the pretense of needing to grab a warm towel for Mr. Mathews, but really, I needed to breathe for a moment. I was feeling a little overwhelmed with the promises I'd made to Parker to tie up her loose ends. Before I even got started on the nursery, I was going back to the hospital to plant another kiss on sweet little Stella's head and congratulate her mommy.

4

GRAY

"There's my big bro!" Grace threw open her front door like we hadn't just seen each other the day before yesterday. The smiles—both mine and hers—were genuine, as was the warmth we shared and the joy that filled my heart at seeing my baby sister finally settled and happy.

"Look at this place." I hugged her and peeked over her shoulder, marveling at the home she'd made. I'd helped her mate, Konstantin, with the building of the home, but it was Grace's touch that had turned the house into a home.

"You didn't say anything about my new haircut, but you ooh and ahh over the house." Rolling her eyes, she turned and waved me on to the rest of the space. "Go on, get your fill, then."

"Nice 'do." I ruffled the new hairdo, which I *had* noticed, and stepped inside to inspect the place. She'd filled bookshelves, added stylish knickknacks and put down throw rugs. There were even coasters on the coffee table. "Looks like you've already lived here for years."

"Just because we didn't learn how to settle down when we were kids doesn't mean we can't learn to do it now. Kon and I just found stuff that we loved on Amazon and put it together over the last month or two."

Saying that we hadn't learned to settle down was a huge understatement. We'd never stayed in one place for longer than six months, and there'd never been any effort put into any dwelling we'd lived in. There had been many different dwellings, too—apartments, trailers, rental homes, even tents. We'd once lived in a bus, until it broke down on the side of the road and Dad didn't have the money to have it fixed. He hitched us a ride to the next town, and we stayed in a homeless shelter for a few weeks until it was time to move on again. Dad was an anarchist but also a conspiracy theorist. He'd been less focused on providing us with a stable home than on teaching Grace survival skills and teaching me how to swindle, pickpocket, and perform other illegal activities to procure the money we needed to live. "Screw the Government" was the motto on our family crest.

In some ways, it probably seemed paradoxical that I'd worked collecting intelligence for a government I'd been raised to despise and distrust, but in other ways, our upbringing had been a perfect precursor to joining the organization—never staying in one place for too long, never settling down, never making friends, and fabricating background stories on the fly.

I'd owned the house on Sunkissed Key for a few years and had never met a single neighbor until Grace showed up on my doorstep worried when I hadn't responded to our monthly keep-in-touch email. At the time, I'd been pumped full of lead and was holed up in Cuban waters recovering.

My sister had always been the most important person in my life, even though before she moved here, we rarely saw each other. The way she responded when she came to Sunkissed Key and found me missing and my house ransacked, told me that I was as important to her as she was to me. We were the only family we had—until Grace mated Kon. As her mate, he was family now.

"Gray?"

I snapped out of my mental trip to the past and turned to face my sister. "Yeah? Where's Kon?"

She pointed to the back and led the way out onto a big deck that overlooked the ocean. Kon was sprawled on a beach chair with his feet in the sand. He looked back at us and waved.

"Water's nice."

Grace shivered. "That water's frigid right now. He's crazy."

"I heard that."

"Of course you did, polar bear." She rolled her eyes and pushed me back toward the living room. "Come on, I want to talk to you."

I cringed. I wasn't looking forward to receiving a lecture, and from the look on her face, that was exactly what she intended.

"Oh, don't look like the world's about to end. It's not that serious."

I didn't relax any. I knew Grace. She was a master manipulator when she wanted to be. Our dad had taught us all sorts of nifty but psychologically damaging tricks. I sat on their plush, new couch and sighed. The aches in my body settled nicely on the thick cushions. "Hmm, nice couch."

"Are you still using that secondhand thing the girls and I picked up at the thrift shop on Main? You still haven't gotten a better couch for your house, have you?"

I stretched my legs out. "Not yet."

"Why not, Gray? You should fix the place up a bit, get some new furniture, maybe some knickknacks. We didn't exactly do a Martha Stewart on it. We were just trying to get it somewhat presentable." She grunted. "It was all we could do to get the broken stuff bagged up and hauled out to the trash."

After my house had been ransacked by the same criminals who'd later kidnapped Grace, she and her friends had come in and cleaned it up while I was still healing and hiding away off the coast. "The shit I've got is perfectly fine for hugging asses. Why does it bother you so much?"

"Because you're still living like you're going to be leaving everything behind any day." She said it quietly with a slight quiver that told me she might shed tears at any moment.

"I'm not."

She sat down next to me and pulled her feet under her. "Gray... Are you happy? I mean, it doesn't seem as though you're putting down roots. It's like you're just living day by day...*and* you're diving back into the same dangerous lifestyle."

I shifted, uncomfortable. "I'm doing the same job as your mate, Grace."

"Yeah, but he's a great big polar bear."

"Wow. I'm fragile and weak, is that it? Thanks for the vote of confidence, sis."

"You're my brother and you almost died. I finally get to have you in my life, Gray, and I don't want to lose you. I know that maybe I'm being selfish asking you to stay here in Sunkissed Key when your urge is to roam, but I want you in my life. I don't want you getting hurt." She hesitated. "Maybe you could work in the office—do paperwork?"

"Grace, come on. I'm a wolf shifter. I'm just as safe as your mate. Even polar bears can't stop six bullets and come out unscathed."

"Six? You were shot *six* times! I thought it was only once. You never told me it was six. What the hell, Gray!?"

Crap. "Look, I'm not going to hide away in an office. That will kill me faster than any bullet could." I stood and shook my head at her. "You need to stop worrying so much."

"Why haven't you filled out that paperwork for Parker?"

I threw my hands up. "A little overbearing, aren't we?"

"S'up Gray?" Kon came in, stomping his feet on the mat just inside the door.

"He thinks I'm a nag, but you know it's 'cause I care, right? I want you to have what Kon and I have. Parker could find you a mate. Don't you want a mate?"

I was careful not to shake my head. I knew that would just set Grace off all the more. "I just haven't gotten around to it. I've had other things on my plate."

"Well, I have a copy of the Cybermates application right here. We could do it now."

Kon laughed and I turned toward the front door. "I love you, Grace. I'll see you two later."

She hurried after me and wrapped her arms around me. "I just don't want to wake up and find that you've snuck out. If you had a mate, you'd be settled, and there wouldn't be any threat of you up and leaving in the middle of the night."

"I have a sister, and I'm one of the owners of a new startup security firm. That's good enough to keep me here." Even as I said it, I didn't know if it was completely true. I was feeling restless. I had been for weeks. I'd been on Sunkissed Key now longer than I'd ever stayed anywhere in my life.

"I love you, Gray."

I turned and hugged her fully. "I love you, too, Grace. Stop worrying about me."

Kon grunted from the couch. "You can worry about me."

Grace's face relaxed as she turned to her mate. "I always do, big daddy bear."

"Ugh, on that note, I'm outta here before I have to do a Van Gogh and lose my ears altogether."

"Van Gogh got rid of only one ear, and he was mentally ill. Don't forget to fill out the pa—"

I shut the door before she could finish and headed down the beach, back toward my house. Cutting across Parrot Cove, I got to my house on Bluefin Boulevard in no time. I'd never expected to live so close to Grace as an adult. It was strange, but in a good way. Neither of us had ever experienced the traditional family life, and I was still learning how to adapt to it all. Climbing the stairs to my house, I cursed the steady throb of pain from beneath my ribcage. Nothing was as easy as it should've been after the shooting. Frustration didn't help, but I had more of it than I knew what to do with.

5

LAILA

*M*y workday at the salon had just ended when my phone chimed letting me know that Dylan was in the parking lot waiting on me. He was the tech guy from Miami who was going to help Parker…uh, me, I guess, really get the Cybermates site off the ground.

I waved goodbye to everyone and headed to my car. I spotted Dylan the moment I pulled into the parking area for Latte Love. He was hard to miss standing next to a perfectly polished, gleaming, cherry-red Mustang convertible. His sandy-blonde, sun-streaked hair was a wild mane around his head. He'd obviously driven from Miami with the top down.

The moment I stepped out of my Honda to greet him, the hairs on the back of my neck stood on end, and a chill snaked up my spine. He flashed a bright, white smile and held a hand out in greeting. I pretended not to notice. Avoiding a handshake, as well as eye contact, I popped the trunk of my car and removed the small file folder of paperwork that Maxim had dropped off from Parker this morning.

Dylan kept that easy smile on his face, but there was something about his eyes that made me wary. He made me think of a predator stalking its prey. "You're Laila, right? Dylan."

"I…um…nice to meet you."

He threw his head back and laughed. "I'm sorry. I don't mean to be rude. It's just the look on your face says you'd rather be sitting under a dentist's drill than meeting me." He took a half-step closer and lowered his voice. "It's the feline-lupine thing, right?"

I frowned. "Excuse me."

"Wolf-lion. Dog-cat. You know?"

Still frowning, I shook my head.

"You're a wolf shifter. I'm a lion shifter. There's always some sort of natural wariness there, right?"

Realization dawned on me, and I felt my cheeks heat. "I am so sorry. I'm… It's… Oh, gosh, sorry." Duh. I was a little clueless sometimes about shifter things. I had only just found out I was a wolf shifter a little over a year ago, and while I sometimes had some enhanced senses from it, they came and went, I'd never actually shifted into my animal form.

His brow wrinkled and he looked like he wanted to question me, but to his credit, he didn't pry. Instead, he seemed intent on trying to make me feel at ease. He dug his hands into his pockets and shrugged. "That file there looks pretty sparse."

I looked down at it, taking the chance to regroup. It wasn't every day that someone brought up the fact that I was a shifter. Most days, I never thought about it at all. I supposed that other shifters were accustomed to the shifter world and the other side of things. I'd never get used to it. "This is all I was given."

"May I?" I handed him the file and watched as he flipped through the contents. "Hmm. It's not enough. If I'm going to create the full database that she wants, I'm going to need a larger number of completed applications. I mean, this will get me started on the framework, but it won't be ready to go until I have more to work with."

I just shrugged. "I don't know if she's just been busy, or if she's been having trouble getting people to fill out the application packets."

He nodded. "The idea is a little strange. Most shifters are old fashioned when it comes to meeting their mates. Seems a little unconventional to do it online—like bucking tradition and all that."

"Parker has complete faith in it, so if you have doubts and reservations, you'll have to deliver them yourself. I'm not going to be that messenger." Still feeling addled, I wanted to get away from him as fast as possible. "I'll let you get shot with the Parker death ray."

Dylan rapped his knuckles against the file and nodded. "Hard pass on that. Nice to meet you, Laila."

"Yeah. You, too." I was in my car and pulling out of the lot before I could even get my seatbelt on. If what I was feeling was my wolf reacting to a lion, I didn't like it. I may have been new to the whole shifter thing, but that was prejudice, plain and simple, wasn't it? I shouldn't dislike someone just because of what they shifted into—the way they were born. Something they had no control over.

I hadn't liked finding out that I was a shifter in the first place, and I didn't like to be reminded of the fact. The whole ordeal had completely thrown my life into a tailspin. If I could wave a magic wand and go back to being just plain old human Laila, totally ignorant of the fact that there was a shifter population, I'd do it in a heartbeat.

Feeling agitated, I gave up going by the hospital and went straight to Parker's home instead. I turned onto Toucan Boulevard and took the second left onto Shipwreck Way. She and Maxim lived in the sixth house on the right, a beautiful home on the ocean built on stilts to keep it safe during the hurricane season.

I parked under the house and climbed the stairs to the front door. Letting myself in with my key, I headed to the spare bedroom she'd decided to turn into the nursery. The last time I'd seen the room, she'd just started painting a few different swipes of color on the wall to get a good sense of how each would look in the room. Excited to see baby Stella's new nursery, I stepped into the room and froze.

"I am going to kill Parker," I muttered the words to the empty room. Empty, as in e-m-p-t-y. No paint on the drywall, no furniture, nothing. Just swipes of sample colors.

With my hands on my hips, I looked around the bare room, still in exactly the same state as the last time I'd seen it, and groaned. She hadn't gotten anything done. I wanted to scream.

Rolling my shoulders, I stiffened my spine and pulled my hair into a bun on top of my head. It was going to be a long night. *Don't worry, baby Stella, Auntie Laila will prepare you an awesome room for the best little munchkin in the whole world.* Then I'll murder your mommy. Justifiable homicide.

Fortunately, the paint and paint supplies were all in the closet, where Parker had left them, and the plastic drop sheeting was still taped to the floor, so I could just get started.

Three hours later, I'd gotten two coats of the pale yellow that Parker had chosen on the walls. The trim was left white and I was rambling on in my head about all that Parker was going to owe me. The walls needed more time to completely dry before I broke into the boxes of unassembled furniture and tried my hand at putting those together. I cleaned up and decided I would work on the next item on Parker's to-do list while I waited: Gray Lowe, Sunkissed Key's most eligible bachelor, who seemed to stir up carnal lust in women of all ages, from teens to geriatrics.

I locked up the house and headed back to Main Street. Gray lived at the opposite end of the island. His home on Bluefin Boulevard was just across the island from mine. I lived at the very end of Albatross Landing, on the water. My car wanted to turn right to head home, but I forced myself to drive farther up Main and turn onto Second Street, just so I could backtrack to Bluefin Boulevard.

Gray Lowe's house had seen better days. The sand and weather had worn the paint on the wooden shake siding down. The beat-up old pickup truck under the house matched the ambiance of the house's exterior perfectly. They looked like the possessions of a man who wasn't big on material things. A whole lot different than Dylan, the lion. His sports car had been so shiny that I could've used it as a mirror.

As I climbed the stairs to Gray's front door, I felt butterflies in my stomach, a sensation that increased with each step up. I paused for a second and frowned. Since learning that I was a shifter, there had been occasions when it seemed I was experiencing feelings that weren't my own. I never really knew what to do with that. I didn't know or understand the wolf inside of me. So if, at any point, what I was feeling was the wolf reacting to something, I didn't have a clue as to what or why.

I had the packet of papers clutched in my fist as I knocked on Gray Lowe's door, ready to get Parker's chore done and over with. One more thing down and I could get back to focusing on spoiling my new goddaughter rotten.

6

GRAY

I'd just sat down to dinner on my back porch when the doorbell rang. I contemplated ignoring it. Who came to the door at dinner time? The sun was already setting low over the ocean and most people were either partying or relaxing. Mostly relaxing. Tourist season was over and locals didn't party as late or as hard as the tourists. I cast a long look at my steak. Fuck. It wouldn't taste nearly as good cold, and reheating was a piss-poor substitute for something fresh off the grill.

"Coming!" I carried my plate with me to the door, so whoever it was would get the hint. If it was those damn Jehovah's Witnesses again... Before I could even get the door open, the bell rang again.

Hand on the doorknob, I inhaled deeply, ready to rip someone a new asshole if that was what I had to do to be able to dine in peace. And the scent hit me: sugared pears, fresh cream, and a touch of cinnamon. My stomach growled, and my steak might just as well have turned to cardboard for all the interest it held after getting a whiff of that delicious aroma outside. Whoever was on the other side of my door had piqued my...everything. Even my brain was a little rattled. What was suddenly driving my senses into a tizzy? Some kind of gourmet dessert delivery service or something?

I yanked open my door to find that my visitor *was* the dessert. Swallowing a mouthful of drool, I felt my entire body respond to the woman standing in front of me. My wolf knew immediately who she was. She was the one—my mate. My first reaction was to be stunned —too stunned to move, much less speak. This was the very last thing on earth I expected. My second reaction was to drop to my knees and thank the heavens for the beautiful angel on my doorstep, so exquisite she could only have been sent from the celestial sphere.

Her hair was so pale a blonde it was almost white. She wore it piled loosely and messily on top of her head. Her pale blue-gray eyes were trimmed by light eyelashes and brows. Her lips...wow. Full, blood red lips, the bottom pulling her mouth into a natural pout. She looked out of place in her surroundings—a snow queen in Sunkissed Key. The contrast between her cool, porcelain beauty and the warm scenery around her made her look all the more ethereal. She was tall, curvy, built to set men's hearts aflame. In a tight black outfit, smeared with what looked like light-yellow paint, she set fire to my very being.

"Gray?" She forced that perfect mouth into a friendly smile and wiggled a handful of papers at me. "Parker asked me to stop by and have you fill out the application for her mate matchmaking site, Cybermates."

What a little demon my sister's friend was turning out to be. I hadn't wanted to fill out her forms, so she'd sent my mate to me.

"I'm Laila and I'm not leaving until you fill these out." Her chin jutted out in a defiant gesture.

Fuck, if I didn't feel every cell in my body realign just to try to inch closer to her. "Well, I guess you'd better come in, then."

I was dancing on a thin line between wanting to yank her into my arms and not wanting to come on too strong. One of us was going to have to address the whole mate thing, but I didn't want to pounce on her right out of the gate like a complete animal. I could tell she was a wolf shifter. I'd wait for her to say something.

Skirting around me, she edged inside and scanned the room. Her eyes went to the empty shelves and then the furniture, which was at a bare minimum. "Did you just move in?"

"Not exactly."

Her head turned back to me and she crossed her arms under her chest. The fabric of her shirt pulled taut when she did, tightening over her full breasts, daring me to look. "Just not big on decorating?"

I looked around my house and shrugged. It was pretty minimalist. "I guess not."

Seeming to remember the purpose of her visit, she tapped the papers in her hand. "Where should we start?"

I had ideas. Kitchen counter, my secondhand couch, my back porch, my bed. I had plenty of ideas about where, and how, to get started. She didn't seem to be on the same wavelength as me, though. Her eyes focused on everything in the room but me. She didn't seem to want to even look at me for more than a cursory glance.

Something about that just made me want to do something outrageous to get her attention, to *make* her focus on me. I wanted her eyes on me, I wanted her everything on me. I wanted to watch the fluttering pulse at the base of her throat go crazy because of me. It was like a silent dare had been thrown down and I was not one to avoid a dare. Not at all.

"I was just sitting down to eat dinner out back. Are you hungry?"

"No." Her pale eyes dropped to my steak and her stomach growled loudly. "Sorry. It's been a long day."

I waved toward the back door. "Go. Get settled on the porch. I'll fix you a plate."

I did just that and stepped outside to find her sitting in my chair, knees bent with her feet tucked up next to her. "Here you go."

She took the plate, careful not to touch my hand, and started to stand up. "I don't want to take your only chair."

I shook my head and leaned against the railing, facing her. "Sit. Please."

Her eyes flashed, but she stayed put. Holding the plate on top of her legs, she forked up a hunk of meat. "I didn't expect to crash your dinner."

"Crash away. The way I see it, the longer you're eating, the less you're asking me about that stuff for Parker." I cut off a piece of my own steak. "Oh, I forgot. Let me get you something to drink. Beer, wine?"

"Do you have any whiskey?"

I laughed. "Rough day?"

"You have no idea. But a beer would be fine, too. Thank you."

I went in and grabbed a couple of solo cups and a bottle of top-shelf whiskey. I brought everything out and poured us each a double shot before settling against the railing, happy to watch her.

She took a long pull from the cup and relaxed into the chair. "I really should be ashamed of how I crashed your meal and then demanded your good whiskey."

"Should be?"

With a sexy as hell glance up at me through her lashes, she grinned and shrugged. "It's really good whiskey."

That ache that had been in my chest for months loosened just a bit and I felt myself lean into her. "I'd be a fool to complain about a beautiful woman joining me for dinner."

She was quiet for a few moments as she ate. I didn't want to break the silence, so I just watched her. To be honest, I didn't have much of a choice. I couldn't keep my eyes off her. It was strange. I'd only just been saying I wasn't ready, and fate goes and drops off my mate right on my doorstep. I still didn't feel completely ready, that hadn't changed, but damn if I wasn't trying to hurry up and get ready. When I'd told Grace I wasn't looking for a mate, I had no idea at the time my mate would be the woman now in front of me—stunningly beautiful, sweet and delicious, and...fuck, I wanted to taste her to see if she tasted like sugared pears, too.

We each finished our meal and our whiskey before either of us bothered speaking again. I found myself content just to be near her.

"Okay, I've wasted enough of your time. It's been a while since I've eaten a meal that I haven't prepared myself. I thoroughly enjoyed that, thank you. Now, I should finish this questionnaire for Parker and get out of your hair."

What? I was completely confused. She still wanted me to fill out the form and sign up for some online mate matching site? I wondered if it was a joke, but she seemed earnest, if not a little eager. How could she not know that I was already hers? She was a wolf; I could smell that easily enough. She had to have realized it as instantly as I had.

"Do you want to do this out here?"

Frowning, I shook my head. "Couch."

She stood up and wobbled for a second before getting her balance and grabbing her plate and cup. "Sounds great. So, why haven't you filled this stuff out for Parker, yet? Aren't you looking for your mate?"

"No, I'm not. Not at all." I grinned. No point in looking for a woman who was standing right in front of me.

I noticed her shoulders stiffen, but when she turned back around to me, her face was the picture of ease. "Well, Parker doesn't care. Let's get this over with."

7

LAILA

I was completely unprepared for just how hot Gray Lowe really was. Sure, I'd heard all the gossip about how handsome, how ripped, how charming, yadda yadda, but nothing could've prepared me for the full-body reaction I was having to him. He was… magnetic. Every breath I took seemed to bring me closer to him. Even sitting on opposite ends of his couch, I kept finding myself leaning toward him.

My wolf was still doing weird things, but once again, I had no clue what she wanted. I could almost swear that she was reacting to Gray just as much as I was. Not that I could blame her. He was beautiful to look at. I found myself wondering what he'd look like as a wolf.

"Need a refill before we start?"

I glanced over at the bottle in his hand and imagined drinking more, getting looser, forgetting what I was supposed to be doing. It wouldn't be hard to let everything go and slide closer to Gray. His heated looks were more than inviting. I shook my head before I could throw myself at him like a shameless hussy. "I'd better not."

He grinned, and a lone dimple on his right cheek sent flutters all the way to my vagina. His teeth were so straight and perfect and I found myself wanting to run my tongue over them. "You're a wolf. I doubt you're going to get drunk that easily."

"It's new. I guess you're right." I handed him my cup and rolled my neck. The day had worn on me, but I felt like I was sinking more and more deeply into the man next to me and as I did, the day was washing clean away.

"What's new?"

I frowned, ticked at myself for letting the cat...er, *dog*...out of the bag without meaning to. "It's a long story."

"I've got time." He winked. "Anything to avoid that thing you're holding."

I felt the strangest sensation then. I could've sworn my wolf was attempting to get closer to Gray so she could rub herself against the man. It was almost like she was whimpering for his attention. I shook off the feeling and dropped the papers between us. "I just found out I was a shifter a little over a year ago. The end."

"Wasn't a long story at all, was it?" He picked up the papers and put them on the ground in front of us. "How'd that happen?"

I swallowed hard. I didn't talk about it. Not with anyone other than Parker. And she and I hadn't talked about it since the first day I'd found out. I could give him the bare bones of it, though. "I guess something happened when I was young that scared my wolf, so she hid. I only found out when Parker told me that I was a wolf. I guess she'd always assumed I knew because, well, why wouldn't I?"

"But you had no clue?"

Shaking my head, I pushed back the grief I felt. There was a hefty layer of bitterness there, too. I'd been normal before she told me. Things had been simpler then. "No. I didn't."

"So, I guess you've had a wild year, huh?"

"Not really."

"You didn't have any trouble learning your new senses and everything?" He'd leaned across the open cushion between us and was staring at me so intently that I felt my cheeks burn.

"I...I've been busy. I haven't really delved into that side of me."

"But you've shifted?"

"No. Not yet."

Gray sat back against his seat and blew out a rush of breath. "Well, shit."

Feeling suddenly inadequate, I bent over and grabbed the papers. "Let's get started so I can get leave you in peace."

He didn't protest, so I pulled my pen out of my hair and looked at the first question. A sense of dread washed over me. I hadn't actually read over any of the questions yet, and I had a feeling I was going to want to strangle Parker even more than I already did by the time I was finished.

"Are you currently sleeping with anyone?" I groaned. "Parker doesn't seem to realize that some things are private."

"I'm not." He shrugged. "And I don't get embarrassed easily. What about you?"

"Do I get embarrassed easily?"

"Are you sleeping with anyone?"

I snorted. "I'm not the one filling out the questionnaire. Second question. What do you imagine your mate to look like?"

"Next question."

I glanced up at him and saw a curious expression on his face that I couldn't pinpoint. "Okay. Third question. What do you like to do for fun?"

"Shoot bad guys."

I laughed and curled my legs under me. "Right. Super spy. I remember that now."

"I haven't had much fun lately. You know what they say about all work and no play?" He poured more whiskey into my cup and grinned. "It makes a wolf go a little wild."

I felt my panties start to dampen and I bit my lip, suddenly wondering what wild Gray might be like. "Um, next question. What qualities do you look for in a woman?"

"Tell me more about yourself."

I tapped my pen against my mouth and rolled my eyes. "Again, this is about you."

"I'm trying to answer the question."

"Funny."

"Next question?"

On and on, we went like that. I'd ask a question and Gray would answer in ways that had me squirming in my seat. He was a flirt, and a damn good one. If I hadn't been determined to get the questionnaire filled out, I would've tossed it and tackled him long before finishing it. I had a job to do, though.

Plus, there was that nagging feeling that I couldn't stand. He'd clearly said he wasn't looking for his mate. Was he a player? He'd also said he wasn't sleeping with anyone, though. That could've been a lie, I guessed, but it hadn't felt like a lie. But then again, he had been a spy. He was probably a pretty smooth liar when he wanted to be.

By the time I got to the questions that were wildly inappropriate to ask anyone, beads of sweat were forming and I had a strong urge to peel off my clothes and grind on Gray's lap like a stripper giving a lap dance. Why Parker needed to know about his favorite sexual position, I had no clue.

When I hesitated, clearly uncomfortable with the question, Gray took the paper from me and read it aloud, a grin forming on his face. "Is it too cliché to say doggy style?"

I coughed. "I think we're pretty much finished."

"There's also cowgirl. I love the idea of watching my mate on top of me, using me to pleasure herself." His voice had lowered to a dangerously sexy growl, and somehow he'd moved closer to me. When had that happened? "What about you, Laila? What's your favorite sexual position?"

Heart pounding against my chest, I felt like I was about to start panting. I could feel a drop of sweat roll between my breasts and my panties were soaked. I felt like I might spontaneously orgasm at any moment. "What?"

Papers dropped on the floor. Gray was so close that he inclined his head ever so slightly and his mouth dipped next to my ear. "In what position would you like it, Laila? Would you take it from behind? The wolf in you crying out to be taken like an animal? Or do you want it on top, grinding, thrusting, head thrown back, thighs squeezing

34

tightly? Or maybe missionary? Hands held overhead, restrained, legs spread, feet in the air, while you're fucked senseless?"

My wolf was whining, whimpering. I'd never heard her so loudly in my head and I couldn't make sense of what she wanted, besides Gray. My own body was melting into a puddle of goo on his couch.

Just before he touched me, I jumped off the couch, straightened into a stiffer, more rigid posture, scooped up the papers from the floor, and forced a tight smile at him. He was everything and a bag of chips, but I wasn't there for that. Waving the papers at him, I scooted toward the door.

"Thanks for dinner. It was hot." I stuttered. "*Great!* It was great, I mean. Thanks." I'd never left a place so fast in my life.

8

GRAY

*L*ast night, it took all my willpower to let Laila run away from me. Every instinct in me was screaming to chase her down, throw her on the bed, and mount her sexy ass as I sank my canines in deeply and claimed her as mine. I wanted nothing more than to teach her all the wild ways shifters could satisfy and pleasure their mates. I'd been good, though. I'd simply watched her go, even though I'd had to dig my hands into my couch cushions to keep from chasing after her. For a man who didn't want a mate, I'd been love struck by Laila instantly. Now that I was under her spell, I couldn't stay away.

It was the only excuse I had for walking into Jammie's Salon early the next morning. Laila had mentioned she worked as a hair-stylist, and I'd found out from Grace that she worked at the little salon across the street from the office formerly known as P.O.L.A.R..

Laila was the first person I saw when I walked in. She was standing over an older woman, her back was to me. She was dressed in a tight red dress with her curves on full display, and I was torn between the urge to rip it off of her and the urge to throw a blanket over her so no one else could feast their eyes on the heaven that was her body. Her white hair was down, flowing down her back in curls that bounced when she moved.

I sat down in the small waiting area, content to just watch her. She stepped around the woman with a grace of movement that mesmerized me. Her hands were quick and precise, her fingers agile as she tossed hair around, getting it just the way she wanted it. She was like an artist.

When her eyes finally flicked to the mirror and she spotted me, her lips parted in the sexiest way. Her tongue snuck out just to pause over the corner of her mouth and then it disappeared again. She straightened and forced her eyes back to her client as she finished.

"Are you here for a cut, young man?" An older woman with hot-pink hair planted herself in front of me. Her hip jutted out as she tapped her finger against her chin. "You could definitely use a little trim."

I grinned. "I'm here for Laila. If she has time in her schedule, I'll gladly take whatever she'll give me." I hadn't meant for it to sound so sexually suggestive, but how could I help my state of arousal when I was this close to the most beautiful woman on the planet?

"I think just about anyone would make time for you. I'm willing to bet Laila can," the woman winked at me, "squeeze you in." Was it weird I was only mildly creeped out by her sexual innuendo?

Laila appeared, her cheeks pink. Her pale eyelashes were painted darker than last night, her lips an even brighter red. The front of her dress was low, showing me enough cleavage to make my dick ache. "What are you doing here?"

"He's here for a cut, girlie." The older woman grinned and patted Laila on the ass. "Among other things."

"Jammie!" Laila swung her hips away from the older woman and rolled her eyes. "Sorry about her. Are you really here for a cut?"

I couldn't help myself. "Among other things."

"Come on. I have a break between clients right now, so I can get you in." She led me to her chair and then quickly swept up the hair clippings around it before putting a cape over me. "What kind of cut do you want?"

I looked at her through the mirror and shrugged. "I don't care."

She leaned a hip against the chair and squinted at my head. "It looks good the way it is, but you could use a trim. Do you want me to shave your beard growth?"

"Don't shave it, Laila. Don't do it." The young girl next to us interjected.

I just shrugged. "Sure, do what you like."

Laila slowly ran her hands through my hair and licked her lips. I closed my eyes and a low moan escaped my lips. I was already in heaven. Her hands continued to stroke through my hair. She tugged gently and then ran them through again. When her eyes met mine in the mirror, I saw a flash of silver. Her hidden wolf.

That gave me an idea. "I have a proposition for you."

She moved in front of me and leaned down to look at something on my head. Scissors appeared in her hands and I heard the snip-snip as she got to work. "Should I be worried?"

Dear god, I would give my left nut to stay in that exact position for, like, a week. With Laila bending in front of me, I could see the full curve of her breasts in all their glory. "Huh?"

She tapped the scissors against my temple and hooked her finger under my chin to bring my eyes up. "Head up, unless you want to be lopsided."

"You could shave me bald for all I care." I blew out a breath. "Just don't move."

She held my gaze for a second longer and then went back to trimming, her body still presented to me. "About the proposition?"

I tucked my hands under my thighs to keep from reaching for her. "Yeah, that. What if I traded lessons in exchange for you to trash that Cybermates questionnaire?"

She stopped cutting and leaned back. "Lessons?"

I flashed my fangs at her and winked. "*Lessons.*"

"What would these lessons entail?"

When she moved beside me to work while we talked, her breasts brushed against the side of my arm and I growled under my breath. I wanted to drag her out of there and fuck her against the side of the building until she screamed. I wanted to be in her more than I wanted my next breath.

"Gray?"

"Um…scenting, hunting, all the fun stuff." I squeezed my eyes shut to regain some semblance of control.

Laila stroked her hand over my beard stubble, she was again in front of me. Her eyes were on mine when I opened them. "Lessons in exchange for tossing the questionnaire?"

I nodded. Her hands on my face were derailing any chance I had of getting a hold of myself and walking out of here without an erection the likes of a steel rod in my pants.

"Okay."

"Okay?"

She grinned. "Okay. Why not? October was right, though. I'm not shaving the five o'clock shadow. I like it on you. It works."

I reached out and caught her wrist. "Just be sure to burn those papers. I'm not looking for anyone else."

9

LAILA

*H*eart racing, I finished Gray's haircut. I didn't change much. He didn't need it. His chocolate-colored hair was sexy in the tousled, carefree way that he wore it. He looked like he'd just rolled out of bed and ran his fingers through it, which created the best mental images in my head.

The man had gotten more comfortable with me and was sneaking little touches. It was distracting and he'd almost lost an ear when his hand had snaked out to lightly brush my hip. Just that one touch had left me drowning in desire. I couldn't remember another time that I'd wanted a man so much. Just the way he looked at me through the mirror while I trimmed his hair was enough to make me want to strip naked and wiggle my ass in the air as an invitation for him to mount me and screw me senseless.

I was shocked that he'd found me. Even more shocked that he'd offered to give me wolf lessons. I wasn't completely sure it wasn't a ruse to get me alone so he could have his way with me, but if it was, well, I was walking into it willing. As for his questionnaire? I'd ripped it up as soon as I'd gotten home the night before. Gray had said he didn't want a mate. That was the excuse I gave myself as I scattered the paper fragments into the trash can. Okay, truth, the idea of him with a woman of Parker's choosing made me want to rip my hair out. He didn't need to know that, though.

My next client was waiting, and Gray was cleaned up and ready to go, but he lingered next to my chair. His eyes were smoldering as his gaze bore into me, and I would have had to be blind to miss the bulge in his pants.

"Tonight, then?"

"I can't. I'm finishing Parker's nursery for her tonight."

"I'll help." He stepped closer and I could smell peppermint on his breath. "Let me help."

I swallowed and nodded. "Um, okay. I'll write down the address for you."

He tapped his nose and grinned at me. "I'll find you."

I nodded and held my breath as I watched him walk out. I swore my lady bits were pulsing in rhythm with his steps. I ran a hand over my forehead and fanned myself before turning to October.

She stared back at me with a shocked expression on her face. "He wants to swing from your chandeliers. Naked."

"Oh, he wants more than that. I bet that man's a beast in the bedroom. He'd come up with some things to do to her that we've never even heard of." Jammie pulled an old church fan out of her station and fanned herself. "Did you see the size of that bulge?"

Kitty shoved the dryer down on a lady and smacked her lips. "Did we ever!"

I buried my face in my hands and shook my head. "Too much. Way too much."

"Pretty sure he's planning to bewitch you with his magic meat wand tonight." October shook her head. "It's not fair. He didn't even look at the rest of us. I want a hot guy to come in and pop a boner in my chair."

Margie wagged her finger at the younger woman. "Careful what you wish for. Old Joe Hill had a boner in my chair last week."

"Gross. I said *hot*."

Kitty laughed. "Old Joe Hill was once young Joe Hill and oooh, lordy, was he ever hot."

"What happened to him?"

"He married that old battle-ax of an ex-wife of his. She's mean enough to take the hot out of an inferno."

I laughed, thankful the subject had turned away from me. I had other things to focus on, anyway. Like my next client. And whether or not I was really going to going to experience Gray Lowe's magic.

By the time the workday had ended and it was time to go to Parker's, I was a nervous wreck. I'd been to the moon and back overthinking Gray's reasons for offering to help me with the nursery. Maybe Gray was just a flirt and really hated the idea of Parker trying to set him up. Maybe he didn't want me at all. Maybe, he was an alien and he was going to beam me up to space when he met me at Parker's. If the last one were true, I just hoped he'd let me finish the nursery first. Parker would be home the next day and I wanted baby Stella to have the best welcome she could get.

The chance that Gray wanted me as much as I wanted him was terrifying. It'd been forever since I hooked up with anyone. I couldn't remember how to even do it, it'd been so long. Not the act itself. I got the anatomy of things, but the slide from standing awkwardly next to someone hoping your breath wasn't stale to letting them release their bodily fluids inside your body cavity... Jeez, I was a wreck. My brain was frazzled.

The comments from my coworkers didn't help. There was a lot of dirty talk in a shop full of women. Everything from penis size to enhancement toys to favorite flavor of lube had come up. I'd unfortunately heard Margie say how much she adored watermelon-flavored lube. Water based, of course. Now I had to figure out how to unhear that.

Halfway to Parker's, I was almost convinced that Stella would be fine if I didn't finish her room. It wasn't like she'd be sleeping in it. Parker had already said she was going to have her baby in a bassinette next to her bed for the first few weeks. Before I could do a U-turn and chicken out, though, I was there.

I let myself in and pulled an apron on over my dress to do a few touchups to the paint job. I listened for the sound of Gray the whole time, but I was still surprised when I heard the rumble of his old truck pulling in the driveway. I peeked out the window and then went to the front door to watch him climb out.

In a mouthwatering flow of well-fitting denim and muscle, he stood and his gaze turned to me. The corner of his mouth lifted and the sexy dimple sprouted on his cheek. He wasted no time climbing the stairs. One hand on the rail, he took them two at a time and only stopped when we were eye level. Still a couple of steps below me, his eyes trailed over my body.

"I didn't think this dress could get better." His finger lightly lifted the front of my apron. "I was wrong. Who knew?"

I rolled my eyes and pretended like his words didn't affect me. "Come on. I have work for you."

Following me inside, he pushed the door shut behind him and locked it. When he saw me raise my eyebrows, he shrugged. "Habit."

"From being a super spy?"

He made a face as we moved into Stella's room. "That paint smell doesn't bother you?"

I shrugged. "It's just paint. I'm around chemicals all day long, so this is nothing."

"Who told you I used to be a spy?"

I pointed at a pile of wooden pieces on the ground. "Who didn't would be a better question. You're the talk of the town, Mr. Lowe. Now, are you good at building things?"

I thought I was doing great at keeping myself together. My hands weren't shaking as much as they had been, and I hadn't said anything embarrassing so far. But when Gray moved past me and let his hand brush over my waist, I was jelly again.

"I'm good at lots of things, little wolf."

I licked my lips and watched as he knelt in front of the pile of unassembled furniture pieces. Denim stretched taut and my mouth watered. I needed to busy myself with something that wasn't Gray Lowe. Turning to a separate pile of wood, I sunk to my knees in front of it and groaned. "Parker really left everything till the last minute."

"I can't say I'm not glad about it right now."

Glancing over my shoulder, I found Gray's eyes on my ass and glowing a bright yellow. His teeth seemed to be growing longer, too. I gulped loudly and turned back to my pile. I couldn't have sex with him in Stella's nursery. That was not appropriate. Was it? Trembling slightly, I rolled the elastic off my wrist, wrapped my hair up into a bun, and shook out the instructions for whatever piece of furniture I was supposed to be assembling. I just had to focus. There was no law that said I had to give in to the heated looks coming from Gray.

GRAY

*J*esus, I didn't know why I was building a crib when every cell in my body was screaming for me to ravage the woman on the other side of the room from me. I could feel her eyes on me, could practically hear her mind running. The scent of her arousal filled the room until I could barely breathe without my cock aching. The scent of sugared pears had never been such a sexual turn on to me before, but suddenly I couldn't imagine ever getting a whiff of that scent without springing an erection.

Her forehead wrinkled and she looked frustrated. "I think I was supposed to be building a changing table, but the directions were confusing..."

I looked back at the crooked, tilting thing she'd built. It sat barely a few feet off the ground. There were boards turned backward, and extra pieces still on the ground around her. I also noticed that she'd taken her heels off. Her bare feet were tucked beneath her.

"Yours looks amazing." She stuck out her bottom lip, pouting, and I felt my canines elongate. I was struck with an overwhelming longing to sink them into her neck and claim her as mine.

"I think you put a few pieces together backward."

Still pouting, Laila pulled herself to her feet and came over to the piece I was working on. "This crib is beautiful. Maybe I could be in charge of the décor? It needs the mattress and sheets and things…"

I stood up and smiled down at her. "Sounds like a plan. I'll fix the changing table."

Her appreciation came in the form of a kiss on my cheek. She hooked her small hand around my upper arm and stretched up until those red lips pressed against my skin. Her breasts brushed against my arm and I could hear her rapid heartbeat. She was breathless as she thanked me and pulled back.

I blew out a harsh breath and looked down at my hand to see that I'd bent the screwdriver I was holding in half. I was tapping into every ounce of self-control I possessed.

My wolf grew anxious as I finished the changing table and the last few pieces of the crib. I set up a few more things that needed to be put together, including a swing and a bassinet. Laila hung framed artwork and pictures on the wall after putting sheets and pink blankets in the crib and hanging a swinging mobile above it. I was barely able to restrain myself from grabbing her, especially when she tossed the apron aside and that red dress was the only thing separating me from her tempting curves.

"I think it's pretty."

"Beautiful." I didn't give a shit about the nursery. I couldn't tear my eyes away from Laila. Tendrils of her nearly white hair had escaped her bun and it gave her a slightly disheveled look. Like that, I could see more of her wolf in her and my own wolf wanted to raise its head and howl at the moon.

"Thank you for helping. I would've been here until all hours of the morning trying to build those things." She finished putting the last few things away and turned to me. "I think we're done."

I shoved my hands in my pockets. "Wolf lessons?"

Her cheeks flushed, and she glanced at the clock on the wall. "Is it too late?"

"Not for me."

She held my gaze and chewed on her lower lip, thinking it over. It probably wasn't hard to see that I had more on my mind than just wolf lessons. I silently willed her to agree, and when she did, I couldn't help the smile that broke out across my face.

"Come on, little wolf."

Frowning slightly, she grabbed her purse and led me out of the house. "I'm not much of a wolf."

I watched her hips sway and couldn't resist reaching out and resting my hand on one of them. "I don't know how true that is."

She stopped next to her car in the driveway and turned to face me. "Okay. So, wolf lessons. What do I do? Eat a small prey animal?"

"I mean, sure. If that's what you want."

"Ew! No, of course it's not what I want. I was kidding! I'm not going to eat anything." Running her hands over her face, she smudged the edge of her red lipstick. "You don't expect me to actually put a small animal in my mouth, do you?"

I grabbed her other hip and pulled her closer. "There are things I'm thinking of putting in that beautiful mouth of yours, but none of them are small animals."

Another silver flash in her eyes. Her wolf again. She licked those perfect lips and swayed slightly. "Oh. Well…"

I leaned in and pressed my lips against the shell of her ear. "Come on, little wolf. There's a secluded place we can go out behind my house to test your senses."

"Your house?"

"My house."

She nodded. "Okay."

Forcing myself to step away from her, I let go and headed toward my truck. "Don't worry, little wolf, I'll make this fun for you."

The drive to my house felt like it took forever, but seeing Laila pull into my driveway behind me was worth the wait. As soon as she was out, I was beside her, taking her hand and pulling her with me.

"Where are we going?" She stopped long enough to take her heels off again and dropped them by the tire of her car.

"There's a marsh between this neighborhood and Main Street. Lots of small animals and things that go bump in the night." I grinned at her apprehensive expression. "Nothing that would hurt a big bad wolf."

I pulled her along, not stopping until we were in the center of the marsh. Big enough to lose yourself in, it was a good way for me to see what skills she was actually using without any nosy neighbors peeping in. I wanted to see her wolf in action before I got too distracted and took her back to my house.

Standing in the middle of the marsh, though, when I looked over at Laila, I saw that she was scared. Her eyebrows were drawn together and her mouth was pinched. She wrapped her arms around herself and looked at me. "Why are we here?"

"It's okay, Laila. I just want to see what your wolf can do. What can you hear?"

She frowned. "Just…you. I hear you and that's it."

"Come on, use your wolf."

Squeezing her eyes closed, Laila held her breath. But after a few seconds, she sighed and shrugged. "I don't know. I just hear you and me."

I could hear at least twenty other animals around us, and beyond that, the grass was swaying back and forth in a gentle breeze. The ocean waves were rolling, and people were talking somewhere farther down the beach. There were things making noise everywhere.

"I don't like this. I can't hear anything else. There's nothing else to hear." She pouted again. "What do *you* hear?"

I turned to face her and flashed a wicked smile. "I hear your heartbeat. It's going faster now. I can hear the blood rushing down between your thighs. I can hear you swallow and the way your hair is sliding over your skin."

With a little gasp, her eyes widened. "You can hear all of that?"

"I can. I can smell even more. You smell like sugared pears and cream. I can smell the chocolate of the donut you ate for lunch and the piece of gum you chewed after. I can smell the shampoo you use, something with coconut in it. I can smell the warmth of your skin when you blush like you're doing right now. I can smell the arousal pooling between your thighs."

"Gray…"

I grabbed her hips and pulled her flush against me. "God, I want to taste you now."

LAILA

*M*y mouth went dry and I nodded. My wolf howled inside my head, expressing her impatient desire as Gray's eyes burned into me. I swallowed and my voice came out a hoarse whisper, "Yes."

My arms slid up and wrapped around his neck, and my fingers threaded through his thick hair. Pulling his face to me, I sucked in a breath before boldly running my tongue over his lips.

Gray's grip on my hips tightened before he ran his hands down to my ass and gripped it tightly, drawing me against him. I tugged his lip between mine and sucked. When he groaned, I slipped my tongue into his mouth. His lips were firm but smooth as he explored my mouth.

One second, I thought I was in charge, the next, I was made aware that Gray was the boss. He lifted me and slipped his hands lower, forcing my thighs up and my legs around his waist. One hand went up to my hair and tangled it as he gripped and pulled my head back enough for him to stare into my eyes.

"You don't need your senses to feel that, do you, little wolf?" His hips flexed and I shook my head as his steel erection rubbed over my panties.

I felt like I was floating, desire flooding my head. Gray was making me punch-drunk with need. Still, I shook my head. I had no trouble feeling the iron rod pressed against my center.

"Tell me what you want." His deep voice was a growled command. When I hesitated, my throat clogged with eagerness, he pulled my hair more tightly and trailed his mouth up my throat. "Tell me, little wolf. Do you want me to fuck you?"

A whimper was the only answer I could get out. It wasn't enough for Gray, though. He nipped my throat and rubbed his stubble against my sensitive skin. Growling out the command again, he flexed his hips against me again. "Yes!"

His cocky chuckle should've pissed me off, but it just fueled my already overloaded need. He knew how much I wanted him. He wanted me. too. "Say it for me."

"I want you to…to…fuck me."

"Fuck." Gray moved then, all but jogging us back toward his house. I held on as tightly as I could and moaned when the friction between us became too much.

Gray swore and put me down. His eyes were burning, the brown now a glowing yellow. His wolf was close to the surface. I should've been scared. I'd never seen that before, the heated intensity, and it was focused on me.

Pressing against his body, I felt desperate as I ran my tongue over his throat. I needed to taste him, too. I felt like I would combust if I didn't.

Groaning, he gripped my upper arms and pushed me away. "You've got less than sixty seconds before I rip those tiny little panties off and fill you right here in plain view of anyone walking by."

Heat coursed through me, but I forced myself to move. Crossing the street, I bent to pick up my shoes and felt Gray press up against me. His shaft was harder, if that was even possible. His hands bit into my hips as he thrust against me.

"I don't think I can wait."

I moaned but forced myself to straighten and turn to him. He bent me backward, his mouth on mine. Tongue stroking mine, his mouth took mine in a way that left no doubt about what he had in mind for me. Hard and fast, his kiss was intoxicating. When he did let me go, I stumbled.

"Get inside." Gray's voice was more animal than man. "I don't have any control left, Laila. Run inside, or I'm going to take you right here, right now."

I stuttered in my movements, the heat in his voice was unexplored territory for me. I felt the seriousness of his demand when he grabbed for me, though. Ducking and running toward the stairs, I took them as fast as I could, my heart racing. I could hear him right behind me. He was so close I could feel the heat from his body.

His big arm jerked around me at the top of the stairs, slamming into the door, sending it crashing open. "Inside."

I barely got inside before he caught me around my waist and lifted me against him. I gasped as I was tossed over his shoulder. His hand slid over my ass and into the valley between my thighs. His knuckle dragged over my panties, both of our breaths harsh.

Dropping me onto his bed, Gray reached over his head and yanked his shirt off. His pants were kicked off just as fast and then he was naked and coming at me.

I made a noise of complaint that he was over me before I could look at his body. I wanted to memorize the lines and ridges of his body, the shape of his heavy erection, but he was on top of me before I could do so.

I moaned when his hands worked my dress higher on my thighs so he could grip the sides of my panties. The material bit into my hips as he ripped it from my body. Panties vanished, Gray shoved my dress even higher and lifted my hips until I was open and exposed to his hungry gaze. I tried pressing my thighs together, the bright light of the room leaving me too bare, but Gray's growl warned me not to.

Sitting back on his knees, he lifted me even higher and then tucked his head between my thighs. The first swipe of his tongue was a heated full stroke from top to bottom. The second was a plunging stroke into my core. The third was a hard stroke over my clit that had me coming apart.

"That's a good little wolf. Give me everything." Gray growled into my wetness, a break before his tongue was on me again.

I writhed, pleasure rolling over me in waves. It was the best orgasm of my life, but I knew there was more. The promise of it was thick in the air. I just needed him in me. "Please, Gray. Fuck me."

My plea must have snapped the restraints on his last bit of control because the next thing I felt was his thick erection slamming forward, filling me in one hard stroke. His grip on my thighs was harsh, the intensity almost too much, but I loved it. I felt like I would go up in flames if he didn't take me hard.

He let go, only to lean down and drag the top of my dress low enough to expose my breasts to his hungry eyes. His fingers found my nipples as he pulled out until just his tip of his cock remained in me. Meeting my eyes, he licked his lips and thrust in just an inch. "You're fucking perfect. Your body was made for me. Perfect."

I locked my legs behind his back and tried to lift my hips. I wanted him buried in me. "More, Gray."

Another hard thrust and he filled me again before pulling back out right away. Teasing me again, he dropped one of his fingers to my clit and circled it. "This is mine."

The words made the fire in me burn hotter. I replaced his hands on my breasts with my own and arched my hips. "Gray, *please.*"

Hearing me beg for him seemed to electrify him. His pace quickened, his hands clamped my hips, holding on. Hard, deep strokes, faster and faster, until he was thrusting into me like the animal he was. My body pulsed higher and higher until I felt like I was one giant nerve ending, receiving everything he had to give.

On the edge of what I knew would be a world-rocking orgasm, I grabbed for anything to get some semblance of control. My nails raking across his back just pushed Gray harder. I clawed and grasped and cried his name.

"Come for me, little wolf. Come all over me and then I'm going to fill you with my seed. This little body is mine." Gray's voice was gravel as he thrust harder, his thumb moving back to the sensitive nub above my sex. Circling it, he held my gaze, his eyes burning with a glowing yellow intensity.

I sucked in air, so far gone that I couldn't draw in a normal breath. Gasping his name, my body tightened painfully until I wasn't sure if I was coming or dying. Then, his shaft thickened and pulsed inside of me, the start of his own orgasm, and everything snapped. A scream ripped its way from my throat as shivers of pleasure coursed through me. My toes curled painfully as my core squeezed, clamping onto Gray, feeling him empty himself. My own body pulsed in throbbing ecstasy like waves crashing over me, drowning me in our mingled release. From somewhere outside my body, I saw myself tossing my head back and forth, crying out his name over and over until my voice broke and tears filled my eyes.

Gray swore viciously, his fingers digging their impressions into my thighs. Marking me, without a doubt, just the way he intended. My body *was* his at that moment—it belonged to him. He dropped forward, falling to my side, his heavy arm on top of me, pulling me against him, closing me in.

I curled into his hard body, an involuntary response. It seemed to be the same for Gray, as he held me tighter and both of us struggled to catch our breath.

We both lay there, waiting for our breathing to normalize. My heart beat against my ribcage like it might break itself out of my chest. I felt his seed in me, his true mark on my body. It was something I'd never allowed anyone else to do.

As time stretched on, the reality of what came next crept into my thoughts. Gray wasn't looking for a mate. He'd made that perfectly clear. He didn't want to settle. I was sure that probably extended to cuddling after sex. I couldn't handle the thought of him awkwardly trying to dismiss me, so I figured I'd take care of it for him.

Pushing his arm off of me, I slipped out of bed and pulled my ruined dress back into place. "I just realized I didn't turn my straightener off this morning."

"What?" Gray looked back at me, his eyes already heavy. "Come back to bed, Laila."

I searched for my shoes. Where the hell had my shoes gone?

"Laila?"

I searched under the bed. Gray looked so tempting… "Thanks for this, Gray. It was great." I rushed out of there. Fuck the shoes.

GRAY

"*T*hanks? It was great?" Staring at the bay of computer screens in front of me, I shook my head and repeated the words to myself.

Serge appeared in the doorway of my new office and raised his eyebrows. "Brother, you're starting to worry me. What the fuck are you talking to yourself about?"

I leaned back in my chair and crossed my arms over my chest as I stared over his shoulder. "Have you ever been thanked for sex?"

His burst of laughter was annoying. My scowl didn't stop him, though. "What? Just like, wham-bam-thank-you-sir?"

Growling, I ran my hands through my now shorter hair. Hair that had just had Laila's delicate fingers in it the day before. She was all I could think about—her scent, her taste, her unbelievable beauty, her crying out my name when she reached climax.

"What's going on, man?"

I shook my head. Suddenly, I lost the desire to discuss intimacies between Laila and me with Serge or anyone else. The idea of him picturing my mate in the midst of any type of sexual activity threw my wolf into a frenzy and had me gripping the arms of my chair so hard, one of them cracked. I growled and stood.

My wolf was tearing me up inside trying to get out and claim his mate, or at least get out of the confined office space and run. He felt trapped. Damn, I felt trapped. I didn't want to scare Laila by coming on too strong but sex with her last night was practically a hit and run. Whoever started the rumor that women appreciate cuddling after sex sure wasn't talking about Laila and me. I would have loved to hold her in my arms, spooning her all night, then maybe make love to her a couple more times before morning. She was the one who couldn't get out the door fast enough.

My wolf was also longing to connect with his wolf mate. He'd seen her in Laila's eyes the night before, the stunning silver glow that was so bright it was mesmerizing.

"That's not an actual answer."

I shoved my hands through my hair again and sank back into my chair. "Woman shit."

Serge snorted. "Are you being literal or misogynistic?"

"I mean it's about a woman, asshole."

"What's that I hear? Woman trouble? In need of advice? That's right up my alley!" Parker appeared in the doorway behind Serge, startling both of us.

How she'd managed to creep up on two apex predators, I'd never know, especially with a newborn in her arms. I stood, suddenly feeling very awkward like a kid caught with his hand in the metaphorical cookie jar. The metaphorical cookie jar, in this instance, being her best friend.

"Hey, Parker. Uh-oh, hand that baby over." Serge was already reaching for the infant, his excitement evident.

Parker's eyes glistened with tears as she proudly placed her tiny daughter in Serge's massive arms. "Sorry. It's the hormones. I've been crying at the drop of a hat. She's just so perfect, isn't she?"

"She certainly is." Serge held the baby like she was made of spun sugar as he rocked her and grinned down at her. "Hey, little Stella. I'm your Uncle Serge. Yeah, I'm going to spoil the shit out of you."

"Hey! No swearing in front of the baby." Parker's hands flew to her hips about the same time Maxim appeared behind her, wrapping his arms around her. "She's got plenty of time to learn all those words on her own."

Parker turned her focus to me and raised her eyebrows. "I hear I have you to thank for helping Laila finish the nursery."

I stood up. "She mentioned that? What did she say about me?"

Parker's eyes twinkled and I realized I'd walked right into a trap. I was a retired spook who'd just walked into a set up a pimple-faced adolescent boy could spot a mile away. "Well, well, well." Parker wore a shit-eating grin. "She didn't mention a whole lot. Should she have?"

Maxim laughed. "Don't try to hide shit from her, man. She's a bloodhound disguised as a bunny. Plus, our entire house smelled of dog when we got home this morning."

I growled at him. Laila didn't smell like dog.

Before I could admonish him, Parker beat me to it. "That's my best friend you're talking about."

Maxim held his hands up in surrender. "I'm not saying it as an insult. Polar bears have an excellent sense of smell is all."

"I'm taking this cutie pie to see Hannah." As Serge walked out, he was muttering to himself something about getting his mate pregnant so Stella could have a playmate.

Maxim looked torn, unsure whether to stay with his mate or follow his daughter. Parker just rolled her eyes and pushed him away. "Go on, go with Stella. I know you can't bear to let her out of your sight yet. I need to talk to Gray about his info for the site, anyway."

I waited until Maxim had walked away before shaking my head. "I'm not participating in your matchmaking venture, Parker."

"I figured as much." She grinned. "And I'm pretty sure I also figured out why. Tell me, Gray, why might a top-secret super spy agent guy like you volunteer to spend his evening decorating a nursery to help someone who's practically a stranger?"

I leaned against my desk, more prepared for her inquisition. "Maxim isn't a stranger. We're coworkers now."

"Try again." She crossed her arms over her chest and cocked her head to the side. "I've got time to wait for you to tell me the truth."

I shrugged. "That is the truth."

She shook her head. "No, it's not. Tell me why you helped Laila. Does it have anything to do with the reason you won't fill out the paperwork?"

Serge came back in right then, grinning. "Hold up. Is Laila the woman you're all torn up about?"

Maxim appeared, cooing gently to his tiny baby girl, who was tucked snugly in the crook of his thickly muscled arms. "What about Laila?"

"Weren't you and Serge going somewhere?" I growled.

"Hannah's on the phone, long distance with her nana."

Parker cleared her throat. "Before you two start interfering in our conversation and change the subject, I was just getting to the bottom of something."

I shook my head and pressed my lips together tightly.

"Come on, Gray, spit it out. I don't have all day. I'm minutes from needing to breastfeed, and unless you want me to whip out a tit so y'all can watch, I need an answer pronto."

Maxim's growl vibrated through the office and made Stella startle and her little fist flail. "Don't make me kill everyone here."

Parker was mumbling something beneath her breath about it being a normal, natural thing for a mother to nurse her baby and that he shouldn't make it into something sexual, but even she knew there was nothing she could say to placate him. Hey, alpha male to alpha male, I could relate.

I rolled my eyes and sank into my chair. "I'm just not interested in a mate matching site, okay?"

"Because you've already found a mate, and she's someone whom we shall not name but who happens to be, oh, I don't know, be my best friend, maybe?"

I stared at the pint-sized rabbit shifter with the purple hair, tattoos, and facial piercings and was tempted to crack a joke about how throughout the history of evolution, my kind would have made a tasty snack out of one of her kind. But it was obvious that Maxim was currently in alpha bear protective mode, hovering over his two females, ready to tear apart any and all threats to either of them.

There was no way he was in any frame of mind to let a joke about one of them being eaten roll off.

"Are you ashamed of her? You plan on rejecting her or something? Why else would you not claim her?" Goading me, Parker raised her pierced eyebrow as she took Stella from Maxim and rocked her gently. She didn't break eye contact with me. She was daring me to let that comment stand. Daring me to let her insinuate that.

Growling, I cracked the other arm clean off my chair. "Ashamed? Fuck no, I'm not ashamed of Laila. I would never reject her; she's amazing. She's smart and caring and beautiful. And, yes, she *is* my mate."

A shrill scream came from the little rabbit, scaring her baby, but she just handed Stella back to Maxim and rushed over to wrap me in a hug. "I knew it!"

Maxim was doing a low growl, and I got his message loud and clear. It was a warning that if I dared hug his mate back, I was toast. Parker just rolled her eyes and cupped my cheek. "She *is* amazing, isn't she?"

Unable to stifle a smile, I nodded. Yeah, Laila was all that and then some. "Parker, here's the thing. She doesn't know. Her wolf…"

The joy faded from Parker as realization set in, and she stepped back. "Her wolf might come out with some coaxing. Some help from a patient mate. Laila's probably scared, and her wolf is definitely scared. Some things happened. Things that hurt her wolf terribly. You just need to convince her that it's okay, that it's safe to come out."

"Someone hurt her?" Suddenly, I was hit with a wave of fury. My vision flashed red, and my wolf's hackles stood on end. No one had better dared to touch our mate. Not now, not ever.

Parker shook her head. "Not my story to tell. Just be gentle with her wolf—with *her*." She smiled but her eyes were cold as ice. "Hurt my best friend and I'll show you why wolf shifters don't fuck with rabbit shifters anymore."

"Language!" Maxim snapped. "But I second the sentiment."

LAILA

*W*alking to my car after a long day of work, the last thing I expected to see was Gray leaning against it. My heart instantly beat out an increasingly rapid tempo until it felt as though I had a big bass drum behind my ribcage. I stumbled on thin air. Fortunately, I caught myself before I took a tumble on the pavement and made a fool of myself, but I couldn't do anything about my warming cheeks except curse them and force a smile. "Hey."

Gray flashed a grin that lit up his face. He looked genuinely glad to see me, and his eyes held a twinkle that made me suspect he knew something I didn't. "You didn't think you were getting out of wolf lessons, did you?"

I made sure to keep a little distance from him as I skirted him and dropped my bag into the back seat of my car. "I didn't know if that was still on or what."

Chuckling, Gray just nodded and reached out to lightly run his finger over my cheek. "Make a wish."

I swallowed so loud that I didn't think anyone needed wolf senses to hear it. Jammie and October probably heard it inside the salon. "W-what?"

"Eyelash. You're supposed to make a wish."

"Oh, yeah. Thanks."

"Come on. Wolf lessons. Back in the marsh, before it gets dark and spooky."

At a loss for words, I just nodded and got into my car to follow him. I wasn't sure what I'd been expecting. Well, I knew what I'd been thinking all day. That I'd put out so fast and easy for him, and now that he'd gotten what he wanted, he wouldn't be back to bother with me. There he was, though. Bothering with me.

As I followed him to his house, I tried to make sense of what he wanted with me—why he was still showering attention on me. I knew he wasn't the dating type. Everyone knew that about Gray, despite the fact that so many women on the island were intent on trying their hand at changing it. So, what was he doing spending more of his time with me? Was he truly just set on helping another wolf get her shit together?

A sliver of a half-formed thought crept into my mind. Could it be that he and I were mates somehow? No, that was ridiculous. Sure, I felt an incredibly strong attraction to him. But so did the majority of the women on Sunkissed Key. Plus, according to what Parker said, if I was his mate he'd know right away. And, I couldn't forget that he'd specifically answered Parker's questionnaire by saying he didn't want a mate. I thought back to all the interaction we'd had since we'd first met. He'd been flirty and playful with me, he'd generously helped with Stella's nursery, the sex had been mind blowing, but he'd made no mention—not even a hint—about anything having to do with mates.

I swore under my breath as I pulled up and parked behind him. He was just being a stand-up guy, helping me out. That was something people did. Friends, but with benefits. Maybe that's what he wanted. Or, maybe, the benefits part was over after the other night. Lord only knew he could have his pick of women, a different one every night if he wanted. He sure didn't have to spend time giving me lessons or assembling baby furniture to get laid.

He was standing outside my car door watching me with a smirk on his handsome face. His eyes crinkled at the corners and that damn dimple was right there, all sexy and alluring as I pushed open the door. "I was starting to wonder if you'd changed your mind."

I forced a laugh that sounded strained even to my own ears and got out. "Just thinking I should keep a pair of tennis shoes in the car if we're going to be doing wolf lessons regularly."

As his eyes raked down my body, his gaze became more heated. That yellow that I knew to be his wolf flashed, and his smile faded when he got to my feet. "Those are...something."

I looked down at my heels and grinned. I loved designer shoes. The strappy Louboutin sandals I had on crisscrossed up my calves and lent me an extra six inches of height. They'd cost me a month of eating cheap hot dogs and boxed mac and cheese, but they were worth every cent. I intentionally paired them with my favorite flowy, short dress because I felt it showed them off. "You like?"

He growled. "You can wear those later tonight."

My stomach tightened and I felt butterfly flutters all the way down to tickle my clit. No way could I have my kept my lips from curving up into a smile. That comment meant the friendly benefits were on. No complaints here. No matter what my stupid heart might want, my head was okay with us being friends with benefits and nothing more. The benefits were well worth it.

"Help me take them off? I don't think they're meant for walking through the marsh." Hey, if he could flirt with me, I could flirt back, right? Two could play the flirty friend game.

He dropped to his knees in front of me and took my foot in his hands. As he looked up at me, his eyes flickered with a fiery passion. "Are you trying to distract me from your lessons?"

I giggled but it turned into a soft moan as Gray ran his fingers in a feather-light stroke up and down my leg. Unwinding the velvet ties that went up my legs, he let the material brush over his knuckles before slipping each of the shoes off my feet.

"Who knew a pair of shoes could be so goddamn sexy? But I suppose it depends entirely on the leg they adorn." He shook his head and gently placed them on the roof of my car.

I gave him a look, feeling a little more confident after seeing that he was affected by me, too. "Come on, spy man. You're telling me that you never had a Bond girl who rocked sexy stilettos?"

He boxed me in and leaned in close to my face, his forearms resting on the hood of my car on either side of my head. "There's only one woman running through my mind. If a woman before you wore stilettos, or mukluks or rubber fishing waders, I can't recall. Hell, I can't even recall if there has been any woman before you. As far as I'm concerned, you're the only woman I've ever noticed—the only one I've ever wanted to notice."

My mouth went dry, my pulse hammered in my ears. I wanted to say something to lighten the mood, but I couldn't think of a single thing. I basked in that statement instead. I let it wash over me until I felt like the woman he saw when he looked at me. If that was a pickup line, it was the best one I'd ever heard.

"Come on, little wolf. Time to start real lessons. No more distractions."

I swallowed hard and followed him back into the marsh. In the daylight, it wasn't nearly as creepy. I had an urge to climb onto Gray's wide shoulders to get away from whatever creatures were surely hiding in the tall grass, though. Gators, no doubt.

"Let's start with the basics. Do you use any of your wolf senses?"

I cleared my throat, suddenly feeling put on the spot. The answer was embarrassing, especially when it seemed most of my friends these days were either shifters or mates of shifters. There were a lot of shifters in my life but none were clueless about their shifter side like I was. I was a useless shifter. "No."

"You haven't been able to master anything in the last year?" His tone was gentle, the look in his eyes soft.

I looked away and shook my head. "This hasn't exactly been something that I've welcomed."

Gray must have noticed my discomfort. "I'll make you a promise." He took my hand and rested it on his chest. "I promise you that you're going to love it. There's nothing else like it. We've just got to get you over the initial hump."

Snorting a laugh, I pulled my hand back and brushed a strand of hair out of my face. "I think we did the initial humping last night."

Laughing loudly, Gray bit his lip and took me by the shoulders. "I set that up for you, didn't I?

"I couldn't resist."

"Okay, Seinfeld, now close your eyes. We'll start with the easy stuff."

I sighed and closed my eyes. "Okay, what now?"

He leaned closer. "Just take a breath—inhale deeply, consciously. Share the breath with your wolf. Let her breathe in with you."

I tightened my fists at my sides and licked my lips. It wasn't easy. None of this was easy for me. Still, I inhaled, thinking about the way the air felt as it entered my lungs. I'd practiced yoga in the past. I could do focused breathing all day long. It was the part about involving my wolf and sharing the breath with her that felt strange and awkward. She was so difficult to connect with. She was just this...frightened animal, cowering, hiding away. She didn't want to come out.

"Relax, little wolf." Gray moved closer, towering over me as he shifted his hand to rest over my heart. "Come out and play, sweetheart. C'mon, girl."

He was speaking to *her*. And damn if she didn't poke her head up. I felt her then, strong—stronger than ever before. She wanted to come out for him. Sucking in a deep breath, I startled when I noticed the change. Scents! The intensity of the scents was different.

Gray smelled like leather and coriander and woodsmoke and lime, a masculine scent that was uniquely *him*. Under his unique aroma, I was able to scent everything about him. He'd showered before coming to meet me, with some kind of deodorant soap—Dial. It was Dial soap. Even so, I could still smell myself on him, our mingled scents, the smell of sex we had the night before.

Then, as my mind reached out, the smell of salt water and sand and mud and the grass under our feet—it all hit me. She was coming out, coaxed by Gray.

"That's it, baby. Come on out for me."

Too much. Oh no, it was too much. Anxiety. Fear. Panic. I wasn't ready. She couldn't come out. I slammed whatever wall there was, whatever barrier was between us, back into place. I stumbled backwards, away from Gray. When he reached for me, I held up my hands and shook my head harshly.

"No, please. I just… I need to go home. I can't. I'm sorry." I barely remembered running back to my car, diving in and slamming the door. I forgot all about my shoes being on the hood. It didn't matter. I just needed to go home and hide. I wasn't ready.

14

GRAY

*I*closed myself in my office the next morning and pulled up a special search engine that I shouldn't still have access to. Thanks to some very dangerous assignments and being in the right place at the right time, there were a couple of people at my previous place of employment who owed me their lives. I'd racked up favors and I felt this was as good a time as any to call them in. Using a government login, I researched Laila. Maybe a better man would've waited for her to tell him everything in her own time, but I wasn't that man. I knew that someone exhibiting the symptoms Laila had shown sometimes needed nudging—some tough love. Other times, pushing too hard could be detrimental and cause more harm than good, and what worked best was time and a lot of patience. I was determined to see that Laila got what she needed. Furthermore, I intended to be the person who gave it to her. But for that, I had to know what I was dealing with. There was something dark behind Laila's being afraid of letting her wolf out, of that I was convinced. Something traumatic.

I'd watched closely the night before as she had slowly let her wolf take control. I'd watched the white fur start to sprout from her face, a slow transition into a snow-white wolf, but as soon as Laila felt herself losing control, she'd panicked. I wanted to help her, not hurt her, but first I had to know more.

The system I logged into was made for shifters, an organized way of keeping up with a group of people who weren't yet out to most of the world's population. It kept track of normal statistics, like births and deaths, but also of more detailed data, like type of animal and any infractions of the law or moral breaches that Uncle Sam considered to have been the fault of a shifter's animal side.

When I looked up Laila Bisset, there was nothing after the age of four. She'd fallen off the radar of whatever shifter monitoring system assigned to her area that should have normally kept up with her. I clicked on the link for Laila's parents and opened up a story that told of a world of pain. Her pain. Reading about the death of her parents explained a fuck ton about Laila and her wolf. No wonder they were scared.

Paul and Nannette Bisset had been running through the woods with their pup when a hunter spotted them. Both parents were shot dead in front of their child. Laila had been present when the hunter dragged the carcasses of her parents off to do whatever he'd done with them. It didn't say. It did say that Laila had witnessed it all.

My heart lodged itself in my throat. I tried to swallow it down as I leaned back in my chair and closed the browser. Jesus, Laila had had a rough go of it. There was no information in the system about what happened to her after that. It didn't say where she'd gone from there, or who raised her. She'd obviously shifted back from her cub form. She'd also very clearly lost the wolf part of herself that day. Her wolf had probably been traumatized to the extent that she'd shut down—receded so far into Laila that Laila had no clue that there was another part of her being that had been completely stifled, buried along with the horrible memories. It was a lonely way for a wolf to grow up. We wolf shifters needed a pack, even just a small pack, in order to feel secure. I'd had a lonely childhood without a pack, but I'd had my sister, Grace. Although she wasn't a shifter, she was steady and loyal. Together, we were a little pack that provided enough security for my lupine side to feel stable.

My wolf was a part of me—a large part of me. I couldn't even begin to imagine what it would feel like to have a separation between my wolf and myself, to be fractured. Being in tune with my wolf throughout my life helped me determine my sense of self. The dual nature of a shifter was important to one's identity, and Laila hadn't had that. Wolf shifters weren't meant to live the way Laila was living.

I had to figure out a way to help because there was no way I was going to abandon her—not now, not ever. Even if she refused our mating and rejected me, she was still my mate, and she was still a fellow wolf shifter who was carrying around a shit ton of baggage and deep-seated issues. She needed help finding her way. She needed her wolf.

Standing up, I scrubbed my hands down my face and groaned. Even the thought of living without Laila was tearing at my gut. Shaking my head, I opened my office door and stepped out to find Parker sitting at a desk in some kind of face-off with Maxim.

I'd been so immersed in the story of Laila's past and figuring out what steps to take next that I hadn't heard anyone else come into the building. The two of them had clearly been bickering but stopped the moment I opened the door.

"I was wondering when you were going to come out."

Maxim snickered. "Haven't we all been wondering that?"

I rolled my eyes. "Hardy-har-har."

Parker's brow furrowed. "Have you and my bestie claimed each other as mates yet?"

Coughing, I shook my head. "I'm just trying to help her with her wolf right now. I...I found out what happened when she was a child."

Parker's eyes narrowed. "Did she tell you?"

Shaking my head, I shrugged. "I needed to know."

"I don't love that." Sighing, she stood up, and I saw that she was wearing Stella in a baby carrier strapped to her chest. "You did need to know, though, especially if you're planning to help her get her wolf to come out. She's terrified."

"Her or her wolf—which one?"

"Both. Just be careful with her. It wasn't that long ago that she started regaining memories of what happened. They came in flash-backs and scared the holy hell out of her. It was like she was having nightmares while totally awake. For the first six months, she hardly slept, and when she did, she usually woke up terrified, in a cold sweat and screaming her lungs out. She slept at my house a lot because she was too afraid to be alone."

My stomach knotted and I looked away. "I'll take care of her."

"You better."

"Want to give me her address? I can scent her out, but it'd be faster to just to use GPS and drive over."

"725 Albatross Landing. Heading west, it's the last house on the left." With a weary sigh, Parker held Stella's carrier tightly to her chest as she plopped back down and resumed glaring at Maxim, although her glare was halfhearted at this point. "When you two do make it official, try not to go all stupid controlling alpha male and beat your chest like a Neanderthal, would you?"

Maxim growled. "It's stupid to want to protect you and Stella? It's Neanderthal to take responsibility for the safety of my mate and my daughter?"

I held up my hands and wasted no time in getting the hell out of there before I got dragged into their squabble. Plus, I had to make a quick stop at Mann Grocery over on Main first.

Laila's house was a cute little beach cottage on the other side of the island from mine. Her front porch was littered with seashells, and the welcome mat had a bright-pink flamingo on it. The door knocker was a little anchor, and all around the place was the delicious, warm, comforting scent of Laila—sweet, spicy, and delicious.

It was a Saturday, and as a hairdresser, I didn't know if she worked weekends as a hairdresser. I pressed my ear to the door, pleased when I heard movement inside. Now that I knew what she'd survived, the events responsible for her fear and anxiety, I was desperate to do whatever it took to help her. I knocked using the little anchor. The moment she opened the door, I wrapped my arms around her and pulled her against me, hugging her to my chest. Immediately, some-thing inside of me calmed, soothed by her soft body held tightly to mine, and I exhaled—releasing a breath I hadn't even realized I'd been holding.

Laila, on the other hand, stiffened. She groaned into my chest and held tightly onto the sides of my shirt. "I didn't know you were coming. I don't have any makeup on."

I pulled back and looked down at her. Good god, how could this woman think she needed makeup? Her eyebrows and eyelashes were paler but every bit as lovely without makeup. Nothing else looked any different. Her lips were still a deep cherry red and she was still the most beautiful woman I'd ever seen. "You. Are. Stunning."

"I'm in my PJs."

I pulled back farther to look at the rest of her. No sexy minidress and fuck-me heels today. She was wearing a worn-looking pair of soft cotton boxer shorts, a tank top, and her feet were bare. "Like I said, stunning. Whose boxers are those, though?"

She raised her eyebrows at me.

I reached down and rubbed the thin material between my fingers. "An old boyfriend's?"

"And if they were?"

"If you want to wear a man's clothing, I have plenty of things you can wear. I'll bring you a whole drawer full of boxers. Matter of fact, you can have any of my clothes. All—you can have *all* my clothes." I heard the sharp tone of my voice, but I couldn't seem to help it. The idea of her in some fuckhead's clothes was too much for my male brain to handle.

Laila suddenly barked out a laugh and rolled her eyes. "They've never belonged to any man. They've only ever had one owner—me."

A hint of a smile ghosted my lips as I pushed inside and closed the door behind me. She was messing with me. "You shouldn't tease a jealous man."

"You're jealous?"

"Sweetheart, I don't think you understand what you do to me. I'm jealous of the *fabric* that's touching you right now."

Her jaw dropped and her mouth formed a perfect little O of

71

surprise. "You came to my house...?" A pink tinge slowly crept over her cheeks.

Fuck, she was too perfect. "Yeah. I came to apologize. I think I pushed too much, too fast, and I'm sorry. I also think I have another way of approaching this whole situation. One that will be a little better than standing in a marsh."

15

LAILA

*B*y Sunday night, I was more in tune with my wolf than I'd ever been, thanks to Gray. That wasn't saying much, but it was a start. Gray and I had spent the weekend in bed. Something had ignited between us, but I had no clue what it was. It was the hottest thing I'd ever experienced, though, I knew that much.

Gray had changed tactics. Instead of trying to make me hear or smell animals in the wild, he'd brought over fruits and syrups. We'd made a mess of my bedsheets, but I'd spent a lot of the weekend blind-folded, learning my senses in a safe environment, often sitting up in bed between Gray's legs with my back resting against his chest and his arms around me. The only tension involved had been of a sexual nature. Gray was right. This approach worked much better.

It was slow going, but I began to be able to tap into more of my wolf nature. With a blindfold, I listened and was able to hear when Gray came closer or moved away. I could scent out different varieties of fruit and determine where in the room they were simply through scent. It was fun. The best part was that the moment I began to feel stressed, Gray kissed me until all my tension was gone and I forgot why I'd been stressed in the first place. It worked for me.

The more my wolf came through, the more I heard her thoughts about Gray. She wanted him. She even went so far as to whisper *that* word—mate. When I heard that, I reflexively tried to reconstruct the wall separating us—the barrier that had gone up as a protective mechanism so many years ago. Now she was going to embarrass us in front of a man who was proving to be a very good, very generous, very kind-hearted friend. She was a stupid animal and thought the first man to pay her any attention was her mate. The last thing I wanted was for Gray to see that thought reflected in my eyes and run. Apparently, my wolf didn't understand what friends with benefits meant.

Sunday night, I sent Gray home because it wasn't just my wolf side that was becoming confused. I convinced him I needed to get rest for the start of the workweek, and I wasn't able to do it with him around. I pretended it was all about responsible adulting, but I was becoming just as frightened as my wolf. Only, my fear was of my growing attachment to Gray.

Sending him away may have been a mistake, though. I'd barely been asleep for an hour when the nightmare woke me. In a cold sweat, tears streaming from my eyes, I sat straight up in bed and slammed angry fists into the mattress. The awful nightmare had been going away. I hadn't had it in weeks. It was my wolf's emergence that was doing it. She brought it back, and that made me hate her. She was the one who made me relive my parents' slaughter over and over again. Every time I closed my eyes, I not only saw it again, but the pain, shock, and horror also returned.

I gave up on sleep for the rest of the night. Too afraid to go back to close my eyes and see the horrible violence again, I stared at the ceiling for hours, wishing that I could just be normal. I tried to imagine who I would've been if my parents hadn't died. I couldn't. I tried to imagine my life like it was before I knew about the shifter deep inside. I couldn't do that anymore either. Not since Gray. I was stuck in some weird, muddled, middle ground that was worse than where I'd been before I started working with Gray. I wasn't a shifter, not really. And I wasn't a human either. I was something else entirely—some kind of freak.

The next morning, I practically crawled into work. I looked rough,

I was sure. My hair was piled loosely on top of my head, I hadn't bothered with makeup, and I'd dressed in simple jeans and a T-shirt. I felt like hell, had a throbbing headache, and the circles under my eyes were so dark I probably looked like a clown.

As soon as Jammie saw me, she knew. "You're having nightmares again?"

She didn't know the extent of what had happened to bring about my parents' death, but she knew I'd been having nightmares about it. I'd had to tell her when they first started because I missed days of work. She'd listened to me cry and told me to take time off until I could handle it. She'd taken care of me.

I wanted to cry with the way she looked at me, all concerned and motherly. Instead, I just nodded.

"Frannie has an opening this morning. Buy yourself a massage. Kitty and I will handle your morning load."

"We sure will, honey." Kitty took my hand in hers and patted it lovingly.

When Jammie saw I was about to protest, she shook her head. "It's not a request, girlie. You have to take care of yourself when this stuff comes up. Until it's better, you're going to have to let us help you do just that."

I hurried into Frannie's room before Jammie and Kitty could see the tears that were clouding my eyes. On days like the one I was having, it was the kindness offered by the people I loved that threatened to break me down. Frannie was no help there. As soon as she saw me, she wrapped her arms around me and hugged me tight.

"Oh, honey. I heard Jammie tell you to buy a massage, but this one is on me."

That did it. I broke out in tears while lying on her table. She rubbed my back comfortingly before gently working my muscles. She made no mention of the fact that I was crying the entire time. She ignored the gentle noises and sniffles that seeped out every so often. When I stopped crying, she handed me a tissue and then held out her trashcan after I used it to blow my nose.

"It'll be okay, Laila. Whatever it is." She stroked my hair and sighed. "Life can be a real bitch, but we're women. We're tough."

I sat up. "Thanks for letting me cry all over you." I blew out a rough breath. "I hate being this weak. I didn't use to be this way. I never used to cry. Now, I'm just pathetic."

"Hey, there's nothing pathetic about a good cry. It's a necessary coping mechanism. Be nice to yourself. We all have hard times to go through. Crying does not mean you're weak."

"I'm terrified. I don't want to be terrified. I want to be bold and brave. I want to be able to face the things that scare me." I huffed out a frustrated breath. "Which is exactly what I need to do. I just need to face it and get over it."

Frannie didn't know me well enough to know what I was talking about. Not many people knew the truth about my parents. Fewer knew that I couldn't shift, and that I hadn't since the day my parents were killed. She looked confused but just shrugged. "If it's not going to hurt you, face it. You can't move on until you get past whatever it is that's scaring you."

I nodded. "You're right."

"Um… I didn't just recommend that you do something crazy, did I?"

I gave her a tight hug and shook my head. "Not at all. Thanks, Frannie. I'll explain one day."

Jammie watched me walk out from the massage room and raised her eyebrow at me. "Leaving?"

"I have something I need to do."

She smiled. "Take your time, honey. Sort it out."

I had no intention of taking my time. I wanted to get over feeling terrified, so I was just going to do it. I'd just shift and then everything would be fine. Simple as that. Except I needed help. I didn't really know how to shift.

I needed Gray.

Heading toward the office formerly known as P.O.L.A.R., I steeled myself against the whimpering wolf in my head. We were going to get over the fear and move on. End of story.

16

GRAY

*J*hung up the phone and stared at it, frowning. I'd just received a job offer from an organization I'd worked for several years earlier. It was a one-off, which would have me stationed in another country for several months, if not longer. They needed a long-term plant. It was a job I could do in my sleep that offered a shit ton of money. It was an offer I would've taken without hesitation before getting burned by my last employer. Even after getting burned. I would've had to face Grace's wrath for it, probably, but I would've taken it.

But now, I had Laila to think about. She needed me and nothing compared to how much I wanted to be here for her. I'd spent the weekend in her bed, in her life, and being together had felt so right. I'd like nothing more than to spend every day with her in her little sea-themed cottage, loving every second of it—just Laila and me in paradise.

Since I'd returned from hiding away on the Cuban fishing vessel, I'd been pacing out of my skin, needing something else to do—some excitement. I didn't love being cooped up in an office like I was today. I sucked at staying in one place. My spirit had always needed to roam, to travel and explore. Sunkissed Key wasn't big enough for my restless spirit.

Even as I thought that, a part of me realized it wasn't completely true. Not anymore. Things had already started to change. And the change began and ended with Laila.

I had to do a double-take when I looked up and the little wolf herself was standing in my office doorway as though I'd summoned her. A smile spread across my face, and I stood reflexively to drag her into my arms, but she was wound up so tightly, I stopped myself and instead watched as she paced in front of me.

"I want to do it, Gray. I want to shift. Just face the fear, no matter how hard it is, and just get it over with, you know? No more panic. No more anxiety. No more worry. I want to shift. I need to get off the fence of being a shifter or not being a shifter. I just want—no, *need*—I *need* to do it." She ran her hands through her hair and looked at me. "Can you help me?"

Her pain was right there on the surface, and the ache in my chest hit me full force. I reached for her. "Come here, sweetheart."

When I pulled her into my arms, she buried her face in my chest. "I can't do this. I can't keep reliving the nightmare."

"Tell me." I kicked the door shut and sank into my chair so I could pull her down on my lap. "I know what happened to your parents. Is that the nightmare?"

Her face crumbled, her pretty eyes red from tears. "It stopped for a while. Then it came back last night. I saw it. I saw them walking in the woods ahead of me. They were so beautiful, my heart hurt."

I held her tightly as her voice quivered.

"My mom had this stunning white coat and silver eyes. My dad was a black wolf, with eyes the color of the night. They looked magical walking through the woods together—his jet-black coat and her snow-white one." Laila was crying, her chest heaving as she fought to get the words out. "Mom… Mom died first. There was a loud pop that shattered the stillness of the night, and then…she was on the ground, her beautiful white fur tainted by an ugly red stain that grew and grew. Dad didn't run. He told me to run, but he didn't. He stayed.

He hovered over her body, and the look...the look on his face was heart wrenching. He wouldn't leave his mate. He refused to live without her. I made it only a little farther into the tree line before my legs stopped working. I was so scared, I guess I just froze. But I watched. I saw as the man came closer and I tried to scream, but I couldn't. I just watched as he...he...shot my dad."

Tears filled my own eyes as I listened to her. She was breaking my heart. I could feel the pain radiating off her.

"I don't want to be this way. I hate it. I don't want to be stuck between two worlds—afraid all the time. I don't want to be afraid. I hate this, Gray. Please help. Please."

Her body shook with big racking sobs that pierced my soul. I held her against me, kissing her head and rocking her gently. If I could have, I would have transferred every ounce of her hurt onto my own shoulders. Watching her suffer was more painful than it would have been to bear the pain for her. All I could do was hold her as she cried, rub her back, and kiss her forehead. I'd never felt more useless in my life. Christ, I would've given my life at that moment if it meant lessening her pain.

My door swung open, crashing against the wall, and Parker appeared with Stella again strapped to her chest. Parker's eyes were wide with fear. She looked at Laila curled up on my lap and her own eyes began to water.

I mentally called to Maxim. *Get Parker. I've got my mate right now.*

He appeared a heartbeat later, wrapping his arms around his mate. "Come on, Bunny. Gray's got her."

Laila squeezed more tightly into me. Her fingers clutched my shirt, and her tears stained it. Her whimpers were the saddest thing I'd ever heard and my chest ached.

I stood, cradling her in my arms and whispered soothingly to her. "It's okay, my little wolf. You don't need to do anything. I've got you. I'm taking you home."

She lifted her head, defiance behind her tears, and shook her head back and forth. "No. I need to do it. I-I have to."

Swearing, I looked up at Parker who was still lingering in the doorway. Maxim stood behind her with his hand on her shoulder ready to provide whatever support she needed. I didn't think it was a good idea for Laila to attempt a shift in her current frame of mind. Parker had her fingertips resting on her lips and her heart on her sleeve for her best friend. She shook her head in a negative response.

I nodded back in agreement. "Later, sweetheart, okay?"

"No! I can't live like this anymore. I won't go to sleep again until I've conquered this. If you won't help me, I…I'll…I'll have to…"

Parker swore. "Laila…"

"*Please*, Gray, help me."

I squeezed my eyes shut. There was no way I could refuse. Absolutely no way. She was begging me for help and she thought the only thing that would help was to face her fear of shifting. I didn't think it was a good idea, but damn if I could deny her. "Sure. Of course, of course, I'll do whatever you need."

Parker swore louder and shook her head. "It's really not a good idea. You know that."

Laila stared up at me with her eyes wide and pleading. "I need to do it. I can't take this anymore. Please."

Hating myself for giving in when it wasn't what she needed, but unable to refuse her heartfelt plea, I carried her past Parker and Maxim and out to my truck. When I placed her gently in the passenger seat, she whimpered and clung to more tightly.

"Don't take me home."

"I'm not, little wolf. We're going to go back to the marsh, and you're going to shift before we go home."

17

LAILA

I stood in the middle of the marsh, staring up at the dark sky, unwilling to go home until I shifted. My wolf was coming out little by little as she got over her fear. I was beyond exhausted. We'd been there for hours, and Gray kept doing everything he could to lure her out. I couldn't—wouldn't—give up. I was on a precipice, and I had made a choice. I had to carry it out.

Gray was tired, too, I could see it. But he wasn't giving up either, though. Bless him. Even though I had told him he'd helped enough and I would continue trying on my own, he refused to leave.

"One more time, Laila. Close your eyes and picture your wolf, feel her. She probably looks just like your mom's wolf. All thick white fur and silver eyes. She's going to be stunning. See her standing here, in front of me." His voice was strained.

I tried. I squeezed my eyes shut and tried to see her and feel her— my evasive wolf. She was there, just behind a veil that I couldn't lift. She was upset, I could feel it. I could feel her resistance. I could feel her fear, her anger, her pain, but I wasn't willing to stop. I'd meant it when I said I couldn't live this way anymore. She had to come out.

"Come out, you stupid wolf. I hate you!" I snarled furiously. I didn't even know what I was doing. I was just bone tired and wanted it to end. She could end it. She had to.

"Don't, Laila." Gray snapped. "She's traumatized. Be gentle with her."

I gripped my hair and kept my eyes shut. "Come on, you fucking mongrel, come out of there!"

He sighed and shifted away from me. "Abuse won't help her."

"I'm just trying—" A loud pop shattered the stillness of the night, and I screamed. The nightmares flooded my vision as a tidal wave of terror rolled over me, drowning me until I felt it melt away my skin and bones.

Another scream was cut off as my mouth distended into a snout. Excruciating pain radiated through me and didn't stop until I found myself locked inside a smaller, odd-shaped body. A bizarre sensation. Sights and sounds were amplified. The appearance of the world around me was altered. I watched somewhat helplessly as I shared driving wills with another entity—who was also a part of me.

It took me a stunned moment to realize what had happened. I'd shifted. My wolf did it. She emerged. Her fear was suffocating. She stank of it—a putrid scent. White-hot panic. Thoughts racing. Broken, panicked, ricocheting around my head as I tried to make it stop. I needed to run, get out, hide, get back into my body—my other body.

The panic was all consuming. I couldn't get past it. Closing my eyes, I tried to picture my human body, but I couldn't even remember what I looked like in my current state of fear.

I watched in horror as she crouched lower, snarling, growling viciously. She was a cornered animal, ready to attack and defend herself. I tried to scream again and again as she turned her sights on Gray. She was too stressed and consumed with memories of trauma to even recognize him. I fought to get through, but all I could do was observe in horror as she backed away...and then lunged at him.

I felt our mouth latch onto his arm and our head shake. Teeth dug into his flesh, strong jaws working to tear, rip, maim. The taste of his blood filled our mouth and I choked on it. Sobbing, begging, pleading for her to stop. Nothing worked. I watched Gray's face contort in pain. Why wasn't he shifting? He needed to shift into his wolf and fight us off. Why wasn't he defending himself? I prayed for Gray to stop us from hurting him, but he just wrapped his arms around us, holding us closer to him as we thrashed and clawed and gnashed and left him bruised and bloody. *Oh god...*

Even when my wolf let go of his arm and just fought against him, snarling and growling and snapping, Gray held tight, never loosening his grip and never retaliating. His blood was everywhere.

It wasn't until he'd managed to get us across the street and up and into his house did my wolf begin to calm. It finally seemed to sink in that Gray was not a threat and that she'd attacked someone she knew. Someone she loved. She believed in her very core that Gray was our mate. Her heart still raced and her thoughts still refused to settle, but I could hear her thoughts screaming *mate.*

Gray settled onto the couch, his arm still bleeding profusely, but he continued to ignore it. He just held us, his deep voice gentle and soothing as he whispered to us. To her. He stroked and whispered assurances that she was safe.

I cried inside as I watched it. No, not just watched it, *experienced* it. I wanted out. I wanted to comfort Gray, to tend to his wounds, but I couldn't emerge. I'd put myself in a situation not unlike the one I'd been in the last time my wolf had control. I was watching someone I loved bleed out while I stood by helplessly.

I tried to calm down enough to form a clear picture of my human self. I begged my wolf to let me out. I didn't know how to get back. I was stuck—trapped inside my wolf. Forever?

Suddenly, Gray leaned down and looked into her eyes. "Come out, Laila."

I cried. Even if my wolf was wrong and he wasn't my mate, I'd fallen for Gray almost instantly. There was something about him that I knew was special. I wanted desperately to be in his arms.

My wolf whimpered and nuzzled her nose, our nose, into Gray's armpit.

"Come on, baby, come back to me." He sounded so strong and sure. He just wanted me back, but I didn't know how.

I watched him, listened to him talk to me, and waited for something to happen. I ached more than I thought possible, but I was stuck.

Gray never stopped talking to me.

Eventually, his strong voice lulled me to sleep. When the blackness finally enveloped me, I sighed in relief, hoping that, if I couldn't return to Gray, I would stay there in the darkness.

LAILA

Morning light streamed across my face and I stretched. The thick arm wrapped around me was warm and felt so nice. I ran my hand over it and sighed. I'd needed the sleep I'd gotten. I'd been so tired. Yesterday was the longest day I'd ever had.

My mind worked backward trying to remember why I'd been so exhausted. When it all came rushing back, I gasped and shot up. I ran into Gray's bathroom and stared at my reflection in the mirror. I was back. I ran my hands over my face and blew out a rough, shaky breath. It was me. Everything was okay.

"Come back to bed, little wolf." Gray's sleepy voice from the other room was tempting, but I couldn't do it.

Gripping the sink, I watched my face as the tears formed. I'd been a mess. The juxtaposition of the nightmare and the amazing weekend I'd had with Gray had been too much. I'd lost my cool and I'd pushed myself too hard, forced Gray into a position I should never have put him in.

This was all wrong. I wasn't meant to be a wolf. When my wolf did finally emerge, she was vicious and wild and dangerous. She'd wounded Gray. She wasn't stable, and if she wanted to stay in hiding, I'd leave her there. I could forget about it all. Just...not with Gray around. There was something about him that called to my wolf and called to me to be more than I was…for him.

It just didn't work, though.

"Can I, um, borrow a shirt?"

I heard him sit up in bed. "Yeah, but why?"

I pulled my eyes away from my reflection. "I need to go."

"Come over here, Laila." His voice was clearer, a sharpness that revealed his frustration.

I moved to the doorway and kept my eyes on the floor. "I don't want to do this anymore."

Growling, Gray stood up and moved toward me, naked. "What do you mean?"

"I mean I don't want to be a wolf. I never want to shift again. I don't want anything to do with it." I sucked in a ragged breath. "I don't want to do this with you. You…you call to my wolf, and I don't want her to come out again."

His growl rattled the house. When I did look up at him, his eyes had taken on the yellow glow. "Bullshit. You can't just choose to no longer be what you are, Laila."

I blinked back more stupid tears and shrugged. "I can't do it again. The more she comes out, the more I feel like I'm going crazy. I don't want this. I never asked for it. I lived a completely normal life never knowing shifters existed for so long, Gray. I can do it again."

"And what? You just shove me aside, just like your wolf?"

Fighting the tears was useless. "I don't want to. I like you more than I should. She likes you… She thinks things about you… It's why I can't do this. I'm sorry."

He shook his head and threw his hands up. Stalking to the other side of the room, he grabbed a T-shirt and tossed it over to me. "Okay, Laila. If that's what you want."

I pulled his shirt on, his scent washing over me. I wanted to stay. I wanted to crawl back into bed and let him wrap me back up in the security and warmth of his arms. But, god, how much more could I put the man through? He was a candidate for sainthood as it was. "I'm sorry, Gray."

"Yep. Sure." Sitting on his bed, facing away from me, his wide shoulders slumped. "I shouldn't have let you shift. I knew it was too soon."

I walked around and stood in front of him. "It wasn't your fault. I begged for it. It's just too much."

He clamped his jaw closed and nodded. He didn't look up at me, didn't touch me.

I forced myself to walk away. With lead feet, I took it a step at a time. I didn't stop until I was on the other side of his door. Leaning against it, I sucked in harsh breaths. I was doing the right thing. At least, that's what I told myself over and over again. Eventually, maybe, I'd believe it.

I found myself getting into my car without shoes for the third time since meeting Gray. Nothing had been the same since I'd met him. It would be a lie to say that it wasn't for the better in most ways. I loved being with him, but it wasn't real.

Gray wasn't looking for a mate. He didn't want one and, even if he did, I wasn't her. His wolf was stable, not a crazy mess like mine, and would recognize his own mate. Gray would certainly know if he and I were mates. There was no point in letting my feelings for him continue to grow, and being near him only fed them. Besides, the love I felt for him came with feelings of great inadequacy because of my wolf. I was never going to be wolf enough for him.

I drove home and did my best to remain calm as I hurried up my front stairs and into my house. Straight to the bathroom, I turned on the shower and stripped out of Gray's shirt. Still, I could smell him. Stronger than normal, his masculine scent—leather, coriander, woodsmoke, and lime—filled my nose.

The coconut from my shampoo and conditioner in the shower was stronger. The mint from my soap was almost overpowering. There was something going bad in my fridge, the jug of milk, I thought. There were cookies baking next door.

I glanced at myself in the mirror and screamed. My eyes were bright silver and my hands were starting to sprout fur—and claws!

My wolf was emerging. Was she searching for Gray, or was she was just curious?

I shook my hands out and stepped back under the shower, hoping the water would do—I don't know—something! Instead, I noticed a spider web in the corner of my bathroom ceiling—every silky thread was crystal clear. I could see the hairs on the legs of the tiny housefly caught in it.

My senses were on the fritz. My wolf was refusing to go back inside. I was in trouble and I'd pushed away the only man I knew who could help me. It was too late to call him back.

Swearing, I finished washing my hair and kept waiting for my wolf to fade away again. She didn't. We struggled—her fighting to emerge, me fighting to suppress her. She was winning. My bones cracked and reformed amidst searing pain until I was lying, four-legged, on the floor of my shower.

Life had just gotten a lot harder.

19

GRAY

"Gray? You want a cinnamon roll?" Grace frowned at me, holding out the basket of fresh, doughy rolls.

I shook my head. The last thing I wanted was food right then. Still I speared a chunk of steak with my fork to appease her. I wanted Laila. I'd been caught off guard by her leaving and writing me off. She was scared and struggling to conquer some pretty frightening demons. I got that, but how was it she didn't realize that I was her mate? Or did she just not want the mating? I didn't know.

"Earth to Gray?" Grace leaned over and put the back of her hand on my forehead. "Are you okay? Are you sick?"

Kon chuckled. "He's *sick*, alright."

Serge and Hannah were seated across from me at Susie's Diner. It was an impromptu celebratory lunch for getting the new office set up so quickly. Celebrating was the last thing I wanted to do. The rest of their group of friends—Dmitry and Kerrigan, Roman and Megan, Maxim and Parker, and Alexei and Heidi—all had prior engagements, so I didn't even have the comfort of blending into a large group.

"What does he mean?" Grace stared at me, her eyes full of worry.

Glaring at Kon, I forced a smile for Grace. "He's just being a dick. I'm fine. We don't get sick. You know that."

"Just *love*sick." Serge coughed into his hand, which did nothing to actually hide his words.

"Oh my god. Oh my god! You're in love? You met your mate?!" Grace threw herself at me and hugged me tightly. "Gray! Why didn't you say anything?"

What was I supposed to say? Laila had wanted to leave after a difficult night and I'd let her? That I didn't even know if I was ready for a mate? That I was still considering fleeing the coop? That Laila had hurt me by walking away? Not a chance. I just shook my head and focused on my meal. "It's nothing."

"Nothing?" Grace sounded astonished with me.

Serge, deciding to meddle and really fuck up dinner, just grinned. "He's considering an offer that takes him overseas for several months."

My sister was no blushing flower. She was badass and vicious and trained to take down someone twice her size. And right then, she was about to turn her viciousness on me. She scowled at me, her cheeks darkening. "You. Are. Kidding. Right?"

"I haven't decided anything." Sending my own scowl at Serge, I growled. "How about you shut the fuck up?"

He growled back at me. "How about you commit to the office, or not?"

Grace slammed her hands on the table. "Of course, he's committing to the office! You're not leaving, Gray. Tell him you're not leaving!"

I dropped my fork and shoved my chair away from the table. "I don't know."

"You can't do that. You can't just leave. You know how I feel. You know how much I want you here. Why would you leave? Why would you find your mate and leave? Who is she?"

Hannah leaned forward and grinned at Grace. "Laila."

"You're trying to leave Laila?! What's wrong with you? She's amazing!"

"I fucking know that! You don't think I know that?!" I hadn't meant to shout at my sister and I instantly felt horrible. Shaking my head, I reached over and took her hand. "Sorry, Gracey. I'm not trying to leave her. She left me."

The table went silent.

I groaned. I couldn't sit there and pretend like I wasn't going insane. Standing up, I kissed the top of Grace's head and waved everyone off. "I just need some time."

Hannah smacked Serge, just as Grace did the same to Kon. "Go with him! He needs a friend!"

If I wasn't feeling so miserable, I would've felt warmed by the sight of the men rising to come with me. Whether it was because they actually considered me a friend, or because their mates had laid down an order, they were willing to leave with me. I really did need time, though. Alone.

"I'm good, guys. I just need some time to think and process."

Serge folded his arms over his chest. "Think and process all you want, Gray. This is your home and we're your brothers. Whatever the reason Laila walked away, she'll come back. Things will work out. And if they don't, we'll be here to help you through it."

Kon slapped me on the back. "We got your back, brother. Don't run."

"Absolutely." Serge nodded. "And I'm speaking for all of us—Maxim, Alexei, Dmitry. You're one of us now. We stick together."

I was stunned. Here I was thinking these guys were business associates and coworkers, and I'd totally failed to notice that in their eyes we were something more—brothers. They actually considered me one of them. A lump formed in my throat and I swallowed it down before I did something stupid like, I don't know, start throwin' out hugs or something.

"Okay, much appreciated but, like I said, I just need time to think and process." I turned and walked back down the beach to my house. Settling on the back porch, I stared out at the ocean. I didn't know if I could stand seeing Laila around the island and not having her. It would kill me.

Grace was right, though. While it might've been easier to leave before I'd met Laila, easy was just a perspective. I hadn't lived near

Grace since I was eighteen. We'd kept in touch, but I'd basically been alone since then. Now, the thought of putting down roots on Sunkissed Key for real, not just have it as a touchstone on my way to somewhere else, felt good. I liked the island. I liked the guys, and after tonight, maybe I'd allow myself to let deeper bonds of friendship develop with them. I liked being able to stop over and see my sister at the drop of a hat. When Grace had children, which would most likely be soon, I wanted to have a relationship with my nieces or nephews. I wanted a chance to maybe fix things with Laila. None of that would happen if I left.

Groaning, I leaned back in my chair and closed my eyes. I'd changed since I left the agency. Their betrayal had hit deep, and I'd spent weeks holed up, going back and forth between dying and struggling to survive. My body still harbored aches and pains from the attack. I felt old, useless.

Opening up the new security firm answered the question about my career. I could enjoy that work. Still, without Laila, living would be just like being stuck out in the ocean adrift, bleeding out, waiting on my body to heal itself, or for death.

I couldn't take the job offer. I couldn't leave. I think I knew that even before I'd hung up the phone after receiving the offer. Grace had never asked for anything until she asked me to stay here on the island and be a family with her. Leaving her would've been wrong. Whether she was ready to commit or not, she was my mate. Mine. And I was hers.

She had to accept both parts of herself. That was the make or break of it. As much as I'd be okay with her being human, she wasn't. She was a shifter. Her wolf needed to come out. A beautiful, terrified thing, it needed to learn the world, accept that she was going to keep on living, and bond with Laila. Laila needed her wolf to show her that we were mates. They both needed to accept me.

I leaned forward on my deck chair and rested my forearms on the porch railing staring out at the ocean. It wasn't going to be an easy task. Laila was just as scared as her wolf. They were both cornered animals ready to attack. Although the flesh had knitted back together,

I still had the ache in my arm from her teeth to prove it. It didn't matter. She might think she was walking away from me, but I wasn't going to let that happen.

Laila could walk away all she wanted, but there was nowhere she could go that I wouldn't be following right behind her.

20

LAILA

*O*ctober leaned over toward my chair and looked at the back of Georgina Bean's head. Her eyes widened and her mouth, covered in jet-black lipstick, fell open. "Ohhh..."

Thankfully, Georgina was nose deep in a magazine with Angie and Brad on the cover and a lightning bolt between them. She was reading about how their football team of children were dealing with the divorce and was completely unaware of what I'd just done to the back of her head.

I carefully put my scissors down and stepped back, trying to view her head from another angle. "Ohhh."

Jammie noticed the two of us both standing back, hands over our mouths, contemplating Georgina Bean's scalp, and came over, a worried expression on her face. When she saw the chunk of hair missing, she choked on her peppermint lozenge and had to have Kitty pound on her back for a solid twenty seconds.

Georgina finally lifted her head and noticed all of us staring at her. "What?"

Tears clouded my vision, but I fought the hell out of them. I'd cried enough lately. I messed up. Nothing to do but take responsibility. "Oh,

Georgina, my scissors slipped. I'm so sorry. I cut a section of your hair much shorter than I had meant to."

Georgina gently closed the magazine and crossed her legs. "How short are we talkin'?"

Jammie stepped in. "It's pretty short, honey, but it's nothing we can't fix."

Georgina met my eyes in the mirror and I would swear later that I saw puffs of steam shooting out her ears. "I told you I was growing my hair out for the Mrs. Sunkissed Key pageant."

Had she? I couldn't remember if she had or not. My mind wasn't running at a fully functional level. I hadn't even remembered to turn my car off before getting out of it and coming inside the salon this morning. October had spotted it still running out in the parking lot.

"You did this on purpose, didn't you?!" Georgina was small, curvy, and normally as kind as Mother Teresa, but apparently, when it came to the Mrs. Sunkissed Key pageant, the woman was cutthroat. Georgina was out of the chair and flying at me in the blink of an eye. Her arms were reaching for me, aimed at my throat, as Jammie and October tried to hold her back. "You think you're going to beat me in the pageant, just because I now have a bald spot on the back of my scalp? Is that it? You're wrong!"

Without thinking, or even fully realizing what I was doing, my fist shot out and I punched Georgina Bean right square in the nose.

Then, we all stood there, floored.

Georgina was probably the most shocked of all. She blinked several times and then took a deep breath. "Oh, dear, I think I needed that."

As she sank back in the salon chair, I moved around to face her and frowned. "I'm so sorry. I'm sorry for messing up your hair and... and...I'm sorry for punching you in the nose."

"Man trouble?" When I nodded, she sighed deeply. "Me too. My husband left me six months ago for Madeline Butts, who works down at the post office, the hussy. That's why I'm doing this pageant. I thought I'd show him what he lost. I kept imagining his face when he found out that he gave up Mrs. Sunkissed Key. Stupid, right?"

I couldn't call a woman I'd just punched in the face stupid. "No, no. Not at all."

"I haven't been eating. I'm starving myself to fit into a dress that I could've just bought in the right size to begin with, and I'm so hungry. I was sitting here leafing through this magazine wondering what the caloric intake would be if I just gave in and ate it."

Jammie hurried to the back while I gently removed the magazine from Georgina's grasp. When Jammie returned, she slipped chocolate chip cookie into Georgina's hand. "Here, honey. Eat!"

While she ate her cookie, and then another four, I assessed the damage to her hair. "I can fix this. I can give you an undercut, shaved in the back and a sweeping wave on top. It's trendy and edgy and contemporary, and it'll look great with your face shape, Georgina."

She contemplated. "Another cookie and a ten percent discount and you're on."

I could've hugged her. "It's free, G. Your next five cuts are free. I'm just so sorry."

She waved her hand in the air. "Women throughout history have done some of the damn stupidest things because of men." She ate another cookie and sighed. "I'm not doing a pageant. I don't even like wearing dresses. Also, my husband is a fucking idiot."

Jammie and Kitty both agreed wholeheartedly. October cleared her throat and elbowed me. "Incoming."

I looked over my shoulder and froze, scissors once again poised above Georgina's head. Jammie took them from my hand.

My nose knew before my eyes did. The mixture of leather, coriander, woodsmoke, and lime could only be one person. Only this time, roses overpowered the mixture of fragrances. Gray poked his head around the large bouquet of flowers and winked at me. "Don't look so surprised. Did you really think I was going to give up that easily?"

Georgina had swung herself around to see what was happening, and my ears picked up the sound of a cookie hitting the floor.

I tried to think of words…any words…any words at all, but not a single one came to mind. I just stared at Gray, hearing my wolf howl and beg to claim him. My heart beat a wicked staccato against my ribcage, my nipples hardened, and my panties grew damp. It was a traitorous reaction for my body to have for a man I'd sworn to stay away from.

"So. Lessons at my house tonight. I'm not taking no for an answer. I know where you live, where your friends live, and I have the words 'covert operative' on my resume." He handed me the flowers and brushed a knuckle over my cheek and then across my lower lip. "Make me hunt you down if you want, sweetheart. I *will* find you."

He left without another word and I watched, open mouthed, until he was out of sight, my stomach tightening with every step he took. Everything in my body told me to run after him. My wolf begged me to chase him.

"Holy shit." October sank into her chair and fanned herself. "My panties just ignited into flames. Matter of fact, they're ashes now. Ashes."

Jammie accidentally poked herself with my scissors and grimaced. "He's a dangerous man to have around. Enough to make a woman a little stupid."

"Oh lord, I'll be stupid. I'll be stupid all day," October said dreamily.

Kitty chuckled and continued working on her client. "Why are you still standing there, Laila? Girl, you need to get things sorted out with your man."

"She needs sex." Margie came out of the back and laughed. "Don't underestimate the healing power of a good orgasm. Why do you think I'm so good at what I do?"

Jammie snorted. "Don't act like anyone's been near that dried-up, old prune cave in the last three decades. You've probably got dust bunnies old enough to be October's mom."

"Oh, I wouldn't say that. I saw old Joe Hill coming out of her house the other morning." Kitty dropped that bomb and then disappeared into the back.

"That bitch!" Margie raced after her and the ruckus that ensued had Jammie running into the back to break it up, still waving my scissors around.

October sighed, still thinking of Gray. "Was he really a covert operative? 'Cause that's, like, next-level hot."

I growled before I knew it and slapped a hand over my mouth. My wolf had been showing herself more and more, and sometimes at somewhat embarrassingly inappropriate moments. Growling at my coworker like a dog wasn't appropriate. "Sorry. I'm just going to get my scissors and fix you up, Georgina."

"Don't hurry on my account. I'm busy carving an image of that whole scene into my memory. That'll stay at the top of my spank bank for all of eternity."

October and I both shouted at the same time, "Georgina!"

21

GRAY

*J*ust when I thought I was going to have to go hunt for Laila, she pulled in behind my truck. Instead of one of her minidresses and sky-high, strappy heels, she was in a T-shirt, flip-flops and leggings. If she thought she was dressing down in an attempt to look less sexy, she was mistaken. I was drooling over the way the leggings hugged the curve of her thighs before she'd even taken three steps. That plus the way the worn cotton shirt showed just a hint of the outline of her nipples had me stunned stupid for a few seconds.

Laila clearly had things on her mind, though. "I'm only here because this wolf won't leave me alone."

I tilted my head to the side and waited for her to finish.

"Don't do that. Don't do that cute head tilt thingy." She groaned and turned away from me continuing on toward the marsh. She didn't wait for me. "Come on. Let's get this over with."

The leggings from the back were even better, but I didn't want to press my luck by pointing that out. "So, you're not trying to shut her out anymore?"

"I want to. I want to bury all of this and forget it." Her eyes flicked to me and I knew she didn't mean me. My ego was saved. "She's not going away, though. She's showing up more than ever."

I watched her hesitate and waited.

"I shifted again. Twice more, actually. I didn't want to, and definitely didn't mean to, but I did. She wasn't so panicked, so I could think clearly enough to shift back." With a grunt, Laila crossed her arms over her chest and glared at me. "These wolf lessons... I didn't know it would be like this."

"Like what, little wolf?"

"Like..." She scrunched up her nose. "It's maddening. Hearing her thoughts and getting everything through her senses... It's intense. Everything is louder, smells stronger, even tastes are different. The perm solution at work almost killed me today. *I* almost killed someone today."

I straightened at that and moved closer. "What?"

"Not literally." With a pout, she cocked her hip out. "I butchered a haircut. First time since I was a student that I had a slip up like that. The woman had a strong reaction, understandably so, and I punched her. I'm also growling at people."

I laughed. "Why are you growling at people?"

"Because October said—" She stopped herself. "No reason. I just... This is all a lot. I thought it would all be easier, I guess."

"It's easy for some people. They just shift one day and their family is there, talking them through it. Things make sense and they fit in. For others, like us, it's not all Leave It to Beaver-esque." I shrugged. "My mom was a wolf shifter, but my dad wasn't. In fact, my dad wasn't much of a human either. When I was born, my mom knew I was a shifter, but when she left my dad, she didn't take me with her. She ran off and left me with a dad who had absolutely no clue about shifters until he had a kid who was one. He called me an abomination. Every accidental shift I had as a kid earned me a harsh beating and a night in a dog crate. I was riddled with shame, and I used to pray that I never shifted again."

Laila bit her lip and swayed toward me. "Oh, Gray. That's so horrible."

"It was. We moved nonstop. He was always saying that it was because of me. We couldn't stay in one place, or someone might find out about me and report me to the government. They'd take me and run tests on me until I died from all the poking and prodding. Turns out, that was all bullshit. The government knows all about shifters. We moved so much because Dad was a conspiracy theorist and a petty criminal."

"You lived your entire childhood with that kind of abuse?"

"Well, by the time I was twelve, the beatings and crating stopped. That was when I had more control over my animal, and I let him know one night that if he ever touched me again, his obituary would appear in the next day's newspaper as 'man mauled to death by wolves.' Anyway, I just wanted you to know that you're not alone. Our wolves aren't our enemies, and they aren't some foreign invader taking over our bodies. They are our kindred spirits, a part of us. They're our other halves. I want to see you accept your wolf and allow yourself to feel that connection."

"What's it like to not fight it constantly?"

I grinned. "Let me show you how good it can be, little wolf."

"I don't think this is a good time for sex, Gray."

I laughed, a full-on, deep gut laugh. "Not what I meant, but I feel like with you around, it's never *not* a good time for sex."

Cheeks red, she uncrossed her arms and slapped my bicep. "Down, boy."

"Come on. I want to do something with you." I winked at her. "Just in case your mind is still in the gutter, I'm not talking about sex. Not right now, anyway."

Grinning, she followed me as I led her to the edge of the marsh, a place we'd still be hidden enough to shift, but could still see the ocean. She hesitated, frowning at me, the worry evident in her beautiful features.

"Relax. You're safe with me. Have fun, Laila. Let your hair down and let's live a little." I leaned into her and took her hand. "I would never let anything happen to you. You're safe with me."

Her eyes were wary, but I watched as her determination won out over her fear. Straightening her spine, she nodded. "Clearly, I was wrong about being able to force my wolf back into hiding. I need to embrace this."

"You do." *With me*. I leaned in and stole a quick, somewhat chaste, kiss from her. It was entirely too short, but it would have to do. "Come on. Show me how you shift, little wolf."

"It's…it's not that easy."

"We've got time. I'm going to shift and sit here with you. When you're ready, you shift, too."

She looked surprised. "You're going to shift, too?"

I grinned and nodded. "I'm not letting you have all the fun."

She settled at the edge of the marsh, in the sand, and wrapped her arms around her knees. She looked back at me nervously. "Don't bite me the way I bit you, okay?"

"I only bite in ways that you'd like, baby." I waggled my eyebrows and as she laughed, I shifted. Seamlessly, I transitioned into my animal —a large, chocolate-brown wolf with blonde patches of fur.

I sat next to Laila and let her look at me. Preening under our mate's inspection, my wolf's tail flicked sand everywhere. My wolf was ready to run with his mate. I was watching Laila for signs of distress. She seemed to just be amazed, though.

"Holy shit. I never actually saw another wolf shifter up close like this."

I leaned toward her and ran my tongue over her cheek. When she squealed and shoved her hands into my fur, giggling, my wolf all but purred like a kitten.

"You're beautiful." When I huffed, she giggled again. "Alright, *magnificent*. Is that better? It's true. And you're huge. You'd never be able to pass as a dog, or even a regular wolf."

I raised my snout in the air and let out a long howl and buried my head in her lap.

"I don't know what I'm doing, Gray. My life hasn't settled down since I found out everything, and I just missed being normal." Stroking my head, she sighed. "We aren't normal, are we? You and I, we're something else. We're…magnificent."

I licked her face again before running a few yards away into the sand. I turned and wagged my tail at her, then barked playfully, beckoning her to follow.

Laila didn't shift gracefully. Not yet, anyway. It was slow and looked painful, but it was smoother than the first time, and I suspected every shift would be easier than the last. Her body contorted and reshaped itself until her stunning white wolf that had been hiding away emerged and turned its striking silver eyes on me. Our first shift together. Awestruck by her beauty and the magnitude of the moment, I almost forgot what I was doing.

I intended to show my mate some fun. I wanted her wolf to know what life could be like without constant worry and fear. Normal was fine, unless you could be magnificent.

22

LAILA

"Just so we're clear, I'm not leaving until I'm good and wasted." I looked up at Mimi and gave her an "I'm very serious" expression. "I mean it."

Mimi slapped a bottle of whiskey down in front of me and nodded. "Got it. Drink up, blondie."

I settled heavily onto my barstool and breathed out a big sigh before pouring myself a few fingers of whiskey. I'd walked to Mimi's Cabana straight from the salon and it was still early, so the dance floor was bare at that moment, and the place was empty except for a few locals in the back corner. It was nice; I needed the space to think.

I was just starting to feel a little tingle of warmth from the whiskey when Grace Lowe plopped down next to me. I looked at her in shock and almost groaned when a telling blush colored my cheeks. I was sleeping with her brother. It was embarrassing to have to face her. "Hey, Grace."

She grinned at me. "Hey, yourself. What's up?"

"Just having a drink after a long day at work. What are you doing here?"

A wide grin spread over her face. "Would you believe me if I said I was walking by, noticed you, and decided that the whole group of us hadn't gotten together in far too long? And that I invited everyone here?"

I took another long pull from my whiskey. "Everyone? Who's everyone?"

"*Everyone.*" She waggled her brows. "So..." She threw an arm over my shoulders. "How's life been treating you?"

I cringed. I wanted to run—hike up my long skirt and beat feet the hell out of there as fast as I could. I genuinely liked Grace. I liked all of Parker's new friends. They'd even become my friends. (It was a small island.) I just wasn't sure I could handle being in a crowd or being social tonight. Everything in my life had been changing so fast that I was left tired, stressed, and my head was spinning. And Gray...Gray was on my mind constantly. Over and over again I reminded myself he wasn't my mate, but how could I not fall for the guy? We may not have known each other long, but he'd been my rock since the day we met. And that was no small thing considering the emotional crisis through which he'd stood by me.

No matter what my wolf thought, I needed to protect my heart. I wasn't at full strength yet, I knew that. I was still vulnerable both mentally and emotionally and I had been spending way too much time with Gray. Early mornings, lunch breaks, evenings, and all-nights. I couldn't stay away from him. I tried—but just when I thought I could, he showed up, almost like he couldn't stay away either. It was torment on a hopeful heart.

"Laila?"

I snapped back to attention and forced a smile. "You know, I'm not feeling very well all of a sudden. I hate to run, but I think I need to get home."

"Hey! Where do you think you're going?!" Parker came in with Stella strapped to her chest and Maxim stomping along behind her, mean-mugging anyone who so much as looked at his girls. "Sit back down and spend some time with your favorite new mommy."

"A baby...in a bar?" I shook my head. "Only you, Parker."

"Hey, I'm not ready to be separated from her yet. Where I go, she goes."

I sat back down, grabbed my glass, and upended it. I really wanted some quiet and solitude. I could have kicked myself for stopping in at Mimi's. Who knew social hour would suddenly erupt around me?

"Why the long face?" Parker cupped my cheek and frowned. "What's wrong, honey?"

I shook my head. "Nothing. Nothing's wrong. How's Stella?"

"She's great. Only feeds every two hours around the clock, day and night. She's about to go to her daddy so you can tell me what the hell is going on with you. You look down in the dumps and that's not acceptable. Who do I have to kill?"

I sighed, the weight on my shoulders settling a little more heavily. "I'm fine, Parker."

"Laila..."

"Please." My voice broke and I stood. Pulling a few bills out of my pocket, I threw them on the counter and pulled the bottle into my side. "I have to go. I'm sorry to abandon bonding time, but I don't feel well."

Both Grace and Parker protested, but I pushed away from the bar and headed out before anyone could stop me. Didn't anyone respect the need for a girl to tuck her tail between her legs and run off to lick her wounds?

I hurried down the beach toward my house, but since East Public Beach was empty, I ended up dropping onto my butt in the sand, facing the ocean. I uncapped the bottle and took a long pull from it, feeling especially sorry for myself.

It didn't seem fair. Why couldn't Gray be my mate? Everything in me pulled me toward Gray. It felt like he belonged to me. He looked at me in ways that made me melt. Yet... I knew he wasn't my mate. He would've said something if he was.

I sat there drinking and pouting, pouting and drinking, until the sun set. I suppose I didn't realize just how long I'd been sitting or how much I'd had to drink because when I stood to continue on home, my legs felt like lead and walking was challenging. With my inhibitions lowered by cheap liquor, I looked both ways, determined the coast was clear, and decided to shift.

I'd been doing it more and more and was getting better at it. The whole process was smoother. I hadn't attempted a voluntary shift without Gray around, but that was part of my problem. I needed to cut the strings. I was far too dependent on him, treating him as though he were my mate or something just wasn't healthy.

I was an adult woman. And a fierce wolf. I had to stop expecting Gray to be around to hold my hand and I had to do it soon before an awkward situation developed. Like, Gray suddenly finding his mate or something. I could only imagine that scenario—me, the needy ex-friend-with-benefits, latched on like a stage five clinger to another woman's man. A jolt of searing pain shot through me at the thought of Gray with another woman, which only served to further prove my point.

Shifting, I settled onto four legs and my wolf immediately lifted her head in a mournful howl. She was just as emotional as I was. I let her take charge like she wanted and she ran down the beach, leaving yet another pair of my shoes behind. A real problem we were having. She didn't care about my things, at all. Dresses shredded, shoes abandoned.

The night air flew past us. Water splashed up as our paws stomped through the incoming waves. There was freedom in existing that way, a freedom I never would've known without the help of Gray. Gray— my life began and ended with him. It was a lot for a man who wasn't my mate.

Just like that, my wolf was running us back toward Gray's house. I'd learned how to control our body, how to take over and take care of her. So, I did. We couldn't go back to him in the state I was in. I needed him too much, wanted him even more. I couldn't stand to see him right then, knowing I had no claim over him.

I needed to do something, anything to get through whatever obsession had taken hold of me. I had to prove to myself that I wasn't madly in love with Gray.

Stupid as it felt, I forced myself to run home and clean up before changing into a short dress and heading back out. Back down the beach I went, stopping at Cap'n Jim's, a cheesy club bar. The music was too loud for my now highly sensitive ears, but it helped blur out the endless whining of my wolf. She didn't want what I had planned.

Another couple of drinks from the bar and I was on the dance-floor, moving to a song that I'd never heard before, trying to avoid people bumping into me. When a testosterone junkie of a man approached me, his muscles dancing with more muscles, I tried to force a smile and remember why I was there.

He yelled something to me, trying to communicate, but I couldn't hear anything over the music. When his hands fell on my hips and dragged me into his chest, I cringed. His breath against my ear—cigarettes, gin, and garlic—was nauseating. The words he shouted were drowned out by the revulsion in my body, screaming at me to get away from him.

I felt my teeth lengthen, and I gasped. My wolf was pissed. She didn't want some yahoo touching us. She only wanted Gray. With a snarl at the handsy man, I tucked tail and headed toward the exit, my hastily thought-out plan crashing before it could even take off.

23

GRAY

*L*aila wasn't at home. She wasn't at work. She wasn't at my house, in the marsh, at Mimi's Cabana, or anywhere else I'd looked. Her scent was all over, leading me to each one of those places. I continued to follow her trail, rechecking each location and almost missed the break off of her scent that led to Cap'n Jim's. There was no reason for her to be there. It was an overpriced, touristy club bar that had watered-down drinks and didn't attract many locals.

My throat tightened when I realized where she'd gone. I'd gotten caught up at work finalizing some things for the new business, then I made a phone call—the one turning down the job offer.

Before I could slip into Cap'n Jim's, the door flew open and Laila stumbled out, her eyes wide, teeth extended. When she spotted me, those pretty fangs faded and her arms wrapped around my neck.

She stank of another male. Instantly outraged, my wolf came to the surface. Snarling down at her, I grabbed her arms and held her away from me so I could sniff her.

"Who touched you? Did he hurt you? Take advantage of you?" I growled the words, so angry I couldn't think clearly. "I'll kill him!"

Laila stuttered, her hand going to her throat. "W-What? I... Gray..."

"Tell me!"

Laila shoved at me. "It's none of your damn business."

Shocked by her words, I stepped back. "Excuse me?"

"You heard me. It's none of your business if I smell like another man."

My better senses left me and before I'd even thought about what I was doing, I hauled her up, tossed her over my shoulder, and smacked her ass. It felt so good, I added a squeeze. "It's my fucking business, alright."

Squirming and hammering her fists against my back, she fought like the she-wolf she was. She kicked and beat on me as I carried her all the way down the beach, across Main Street, and up the stairs to my front door. I only put her down so I could sit on the couch and pull her onto my lap.

She continued to squirm, but I held her tight. "I'll fucking kill you for that!" Laila fought harder. "You have no right!"

I held her wrists tight, restraining them, then growled inches from her face. "I have every right. You hear me? Every single right."

When I let her up, she swung at me and only missed because I moved. Her open hand came at me again, but I caught her and pulled her back across my lap, facing me. She struggled, her eyes blazing.

"You let some asshole put his hands on you. I can smell him all over you and I want to fucking rip his head off his shoulders. You do that shit again and you're going to get someone killed, Laila."

"Are you crazy? Why the fuck...? What do you...? Ugh!" She managed to get one of her arms free and tugged at my hair, she pulled my head to the side and I let her, exposing my neck to her. Her very human teeth were there, then, scraping across my throat, marking me in her own way. "I hate you."

I shook her lightly, getting more of my hair tugged at. "Say that again and I'm going to turn you over my knee, little wolf, and spank your ass again."

"I hate you! I hate you, I hate you, I hate you!" Her grip in my hair stopped tugging, her nails raking over my scalp as she grabbed my head. Her body straddled mine, her thighs squeezing my hips. "I fucking hate you so much."

I caught her chin in my hand and forced her to look at me. "You don't hate me."

Growling, she tried to get free. "I do. You make me crazy and it's not fair."

"Tell me the truth, little wolf. Tell me how you really feel." I held her gaze, daring her to tell me the words I desperately wanted to hear from her. My chest throbbed, my stomach was stuck between sinking to my feet and lodging in my throat. "Tell me."

"I can't. It doesn't matter." She went still. Then laughed a hollow, humorless laugh. "Can't you tell? Do I really need to say it? I love you, but it doesn't matter."

I fought a smile, my body releasing tension I'd been holding for too long. She loved me.

"Why are you smiling? Is that funny?" She slapped my chest and growled. "It's funny that I love you? It's funny that I fell for someone who isn't my mate?"

I yanked her closer to my chest and growled against her mouth. "Who said I'm not your mate?"

Laila's fingers tightened on my chest. Her heart beat so hard that a normal human could've heard it. "What?"

I shrugged, acting like my entire life—my entire world—wasn't riding on her loving me forever. "Who said that I'm not your mate, Laila?"

"You did... You said you weren't looking for a mate."

"Didn't really need to when she showed up at my front door."

"You... What? You didn't say anything. You didn't say anything about it, Gray. Don't joke about this. Please don't."

I wrapped my arms around her waist and held on. "I was waiting for you and your wolf to work things out. I was giving you time to heal and decide whether you wanted to be with me."

"My wolf has been screaming at me over you since the beginning. I thought she was crazy." Laila blinked back tears. "Why didn't you say anything?!"

"I had reasons. Although...they seem a little lame now." I buried my face in her neck and groaned. "What were you doing out tonight, little wolf?"

She shook against me. "I thought I was setting myself up for a huge crash and burn. I was afraid you'd find your mate and I'd be alone and abandoned, but I had a hard time letting go. I wanted to find someone to help me forget you."

Growling, I sat up straight. "And you let someone else touch you?"

"It just happened. As soon as he did, I got out of there." She shook her head. "I didn't know why I was feeling this way about you, Gray. I thought I was all screwed up. You should've told me! You should've let me know."

I fought to restrain my fury at the idea of someone else touching her. "Tell me again how you feel about me."

"Tell me again why you kept this a secret from me."

"I don't really know. But I know I would do anything to keep from losing you. I'm not ready to ever smell another man on you, ever again. I love you, little wolf."

She crossed her arms over her chest and leaned back. "Tell me again."

"I love you."

"Again."

"I love you."

"Spank me again and I'll castrate you."

I sighed. "You'd better get this dress off, then. Every time I catch a whiff of that asshole, I feel like doing it all over again."

"Tell me one more time."

"I fucking love you, Laila. You're my mate. I'm going to love you for eternity and then some. That's a promise, sweetheart."

Sinking against my chest, she smiled. "Okay, thanks."

"Thanks?" I growled.

"Yep. Thanks."

Pulling her over my knee, I slapped her ass, laughing as she shouted at me. "Tell me, little wolf."

"I hate you!"

"What did you say? Smack my ass again?"

She laughed then, her voice lighter than I'd ever heard it. "I love you, Gray Lowe."

24

LAILA

"Shift, Laila. Run with me." Gray pulled me back up against his chest and kissed me hard. His mouth tasted even sweeter, now that I knew he was my mate.

I bit my lip and nodded. I rolled out of bed, stood and grinned down at him. "I'm getting faster. You won't catch me this time."

His eyes flashed yellow and he growled low and menacing. "Better run, little wolf."

I ran to the back door, threw it open, and leaped, shifting in mid-air before taking off down the stairs and down the beach. My heart pounding, my body lighter than I ever remembered feeling, I ran for all I was worth. I felt different. Everything felt different now that Gray was mine. There would be no other woman coming between us.

I really should have known, though. Who else could my mate be but the man that who would stand beside me through thick and thin, fight for me and hold me up when I couldn't stand on my own?

It wasn't long before I heard Gray gaining on me. He was larger, stronger, and faster than I was, but I liked running from him, anyway. I was getting faster and, who knew, I might just outrun him one day. I didn't really want to outrun him tonight, though. I was hoping to be caught.

Just as I felt his breath on my tail, I cut sideways and then back toward his house. Gray's teeth nipped my tail playfully, nearly toppling me. He yelped at me and raced toward me even harder. I'd just gotten to his steps, my little home base, when he tackled me. At the bottom of his stairs, he shifted back and rested under me, his eyes intense.

"Listen here, little wolf." He stared into my wolf's eyes, into my soul, and stroked my coat. "You will always be safe with me. I am yours and you are mine. I'll never let anything happen to you. I would kill an army of men to make sure you never get a single scratch. I would cut off my own arm to make you smile, if that's what it took. Do you hear me?"

My wolf tilted her head back and let out a long howl. She dipped her head and nuzzled Gray's chest before retreating—seamlessly—and I found myself naked on top of an also naked Gray.

There together under the moonlight, I felt everything inside of me come together into alignment. He was the man I was supposed to spend the rest of my life with, and I'd found him.

"Let me claim you, Laila. Say yes."

I braced my hands in the sand on either side of his head and looked into his eyes, the intense love he had for me was so evident. I couldn't believe I hadn't recognized it before. "Yes."

He kissed me then, taking his time, making love to my mouth. His tongue stroked mine, his hands roamed my body until I was liquid against him. "I have to mark you. I have to."

I moaned and forced myself to roll off him. Moving toward the stairs, I only got two steps up when Gray was against me. Hands roaming up to my bare breasts, he growled into my neck. I fought the urge to let him take me right there. "Inside."

Lifting me and carrying me up the steps, I gasped when he slammed the door shut behind us and had me bent over the couch in seconds. I was still getting my breath when he entered me from behind.

Filling and stretching me, his cock was hot and rock hard. His thighs against mine were sandy, his hands on my back rough. He wrapped one arm around my waist and his other hand gripped my shoulder, holding me against him as he pulled out and thrust back into me hard.

I clawed at his arm, already lost in the wildness that was Gray. Rough and rugged around the edges, he made me forget everything I'd ever thought I knew about myself. Insecurities were forgotten when he took me with such hunger.

Thrusting into me again, harder, Gray swore and pulled me up so he hit a deeper spot, a spot that instantly sent an orgasm ripping through me. My body trembled and shook, but he continued to fuck me through it. Holding me tightly he ran his teeth over my neck and shoulder.

"*Mine*. You're mine, Laila. Mine, little white wolf. Every part of you. All of you." His voice was rough, his wolf right there at the surface. "We're going to grow old together. I'm going to spend the rest of my life right here. Buried in you, loving you, making love to you, pleasuring you, making you scream my name, and holding you in my arms as I watch you fall asleep. Say yes."

I DROPPED my head back onto his chest and moaned louder. I was barely holding on to lucidity, already riding the edge of another orgasm. "Say yes? What's the question?"

"Marry me."

I jerked in surprise just as Gray sank his teeth into my neck. Wild, ripping, mind-altering pleasure shot through my body at the speed of a bullet. I screamed for him, begged him for more, and throbbed around him as he emptied himself in me. I was there one moment and then I was floating in another dimension.

I lost track of when my orgasm finally calmed into something more on the earthly plane. The aftershocks were bigger than any orgasm I'd ever experienced before I met Gray. When they finally ended, Gray carried me into the bathroom and sank with me into his too-small tub, hot water running around us. I curled up and melted against him. My body had gone to mush after what he'd just done to it.

Gray was stroking a bar of soap over my arms and neck when the ability to speak came back to me. I mumbled a few words before stopping and starting over. "That wasn't a question."

Hands stilling, Gray grunted. "Say yes anyway."

I smiled to myself and lifted my arm in a silent suggestion that he wash the rest of me. "You're super bossy."

He grunted again but kept washing me.

"And you spanked me." I sighed as his hands cleaned my breasts. "You're demanding. And you haven't told me anything about your past. For all I know, I won't be your first wife."

"*Laila.*" The way he growled my name showed his impatience, but also his nervousness.

I glanced up at him and grinned. "Yes."

He grabbed my chin and kissed me hard enough to bruise my lips. "Say yes."

"Yes. I'll marry you." I laughed at the way his eyes lit up. "As long as I'm not the third or fourth, wife."

"Only you, little wolf." He ran his tongue over the spot where he'd sunk his teeth and left a claiming mark. He groaned when I shivered. "Only you."

Later that night, as I laid on Gray's chest and he stroked my hair, I smiled as I thought of the day he and I met.

"What are you thinking?"

"I was thinking of how if it wasn't for Cybermates, you and I might not be here together right now. Which means technically, we're Parker's first mate matchup. We owe her, like, a gift basket or something, at least."

"I'm going to send Parker the biggest carrot I can find." Gray shifted under me and brushed a strand of hair from my cheek.

I laughed. "You're so gonna piss her off with that idea."

"Don't care. That bunny deserves a carrot."

I tucked my head under his chin and sighed happily. "She deserves more than a carrot. We should name our first born child after her."

I paused. "There's something else, Gray."

He stroked my back and kissed the top of my head. "Tell me, little wolf."

"Say yes."

He laughed. "Yes. Now you mind telling me what I just answered yes to?"

"It's my turn to claim you."

With a moan, Gray wrapped his arms around me and held on tighter. "In that case, hell yes!"

Laughing, I kissed his neck and started another round of love-making that lasted through the night and well into the morning.

THE END

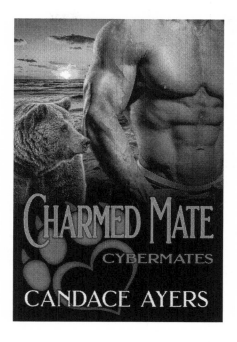

Fern Day is barely holding it together most days. The single, fully-human mom of a fifteen-year-old-shifter-with-an-attitude has no time for herself. Her life is chaos, she's a hot mess, and her daughter is her first priority.

Sunkissed Key's handsome pediatrician sure is tempting, though. When he offers to teach her daughter how to handle her animal side, Fern can't refuse. But that's not his only offer Fern can't refuse.

Harrison Daniels knows Fern is his the moment he lays eyes on her. He also knows she's not ready to learn about shifter mating. She'll only view him as another responsibility, and lord knows she's juggling enough of those already. That child of hers is an unholy terror.

Harrison has his work cut out for him. He not only has to convince Fern that he's in her life forever, he also has to gain the approval of her spawn from hell. Good thing Harrison never backs down from a challenge. Bring it on.

Get Charmed Mate HERE

P.O.L.A.R.

P.O.L.A.R. (Private Ops: League Arctic Rescue) is a specialized, private operations task force—a maritime unit of polar bear shifters. Part of a worldwide, clandestine army comprised of the best of the best shifters, P.O.L.A.R.'s home base is Siberia...until the team pisses somebody off and gets re-assigned to Sunkissed Key, Florida and these arctic shifters suddenly find themselves surrounded by sun, sand, flip-flops and palm trees.

1. Rescue Bear
2. Hero Bear
3. Covert Bear
4. Tactical Bear
5. Royal Bear

BEARS OF BURDEN

In the southwestern town of Burden, Texas, good ol' bears Hawthorne, Wyatt, Hutch, Sterling, and Sam, and Matt are livin' easy. Beer flows freely, and pretty women are abundant. The last thing the shifters of Burden are thinking about is finding a mate or settling down. But, fate has its own plan...

1. Thorn
2. Wyatt
3. Hutch
4. Sterling
5. Sam
6. Matt

OTHER BOOKS FROM CANDACE AYERS...

SHIFTERS OF HELL'S CORNER

In the late 1800's, on a homestead in New Mexico, a female shifter named Helen Cartwright, widowed under mysterious circumstances, knew there was power in the feminine bonds of sisterhood. She provided an oasis for those like herself, women who had been dealt the short end of the stick. Like magic, women have flocked to the tiny town of Helen's Corner ever since. Although, nowadays, some call the town by another name, ***Hell's Crazy Corner.***

1. Wolf Boss
2. Wolf Detective
3. Wolf Soldier
4. Bear Outlaw
5. Wolf Purebred

DRAGONS OF THE BAYOU

Something's lurking in the swamplands of the Deep South. Massive creatures exiled from their home. For each, his only salvation is to find his one true mate.

1. Fire Breathing Beast
2. Fire Breathing Cezar
3. Fire Breathing Blaise
4. Fire Breathing Remy
5. Fire Breathing Armand
6. Fire Breathing Ovide

RANCHER BEARS

When the patriarch of the Long family dies, he leaves a will that has each of his five son's scrambling to find a mate. Underneath it all, they find that family is what matters most.

1. Rancher Bear's Baby
2. Rancher Bear's Mail Order Mate
3. Rancher Bear's Surprise Package
4. Rancher Bear's Secret
5. Rancher Bear's Desire
6. Rancher Bears' Merry Christmas

Rancher Bears Complete Box Set

KODIAK ISLAND SHIFTERS

On Port Ursa in Kodiak Island Alaska, the Sterling brothers are kind of a big deal.
They own a nationwide chain of outfitter retail stores that they grew from their father's little backwoods camping supply shop.
The only thing missing from the hot bear shifters' lives are mates! But, not for long...

1. Billionaire Bear's Bride (COLTON)
2. The Bear's Flamingo Bride (WYATT)
3. Military Bear's Mate (TUCKER)

SHIFTERS OF DENVER

Nathan: Billionaire Bear- A matchmaker meets her match.
Byron: Heartbreaker Bear- A sexy heartbreaker with eyes for just one woman.
Xavier: Bad Bear - She's a good girl. He's a bad bear.

1. Nathan: Billionaire Bear
2. Byron: Heartbreaker Bear
3. Xavier: Bad Bear

Shifters of Denver Complete Box Set

Made in the USA
Monee, IL
22 June 2021

72064075R00079